Fresh from the Fountain

English Writing in Luxembourg
2018

edited by
Anne-Marie Reuter, Jeff Thill, Nathalie Jacoby

Contents

FONDS
CULTUREL
NATIONAL

Published with the support of the
National Cultural Fund, Luxembourg

Preface

Black Fountain Anthology – too grand a title? Notes from the Black Fountain – too dismissive? What lies behind the project of this collection, or album, or compilation, is the wish to group together within one publication a variety of authors who have made Luxembourg their home or English their language. To show how rich and vibrant the English-speaking and -writing landscape is in a country that includes an increasingly high number of expats and that is witnessing a small explosion of writing in English. While the reasons for the expats' choice of Luxembourg as a home are generally linked to professional decisions, the motivation for Luxembourgers to choose English as their literary language is less clear. Some of them studied in the UK, in Ireland or in the USA, others come from bilingual backgrounds, still others opt for English as the most suitable language for their stories or poems. They write about English being their home, or sometimes an escape from home, and indeed the theme of home keeps popping up more or less directly in the texts of both expats and Luxembourgers.

How can a foreign language become a home? When does a foreign country become a home? Or, conversely, when do the original language or home become foreign places? These are exciting questions for research. Native English speakers do not generally find themselves confronted with the question of a choice of language – they move within the world language to begin with. For non-native writers, the choice of a foreign literary language often goes back to transformative first contacts with English – the love of a person, a people, a culture, a literature, and by extension the shaping of a personal world through memories and associations. Since home means comfort, privacy, intimacy, the choice of a literary home is bound to include irrational factors like relief, pleasure, happiness or a sense of belonging. Home is the place where the self can safely be self.

While the topic of home is lurking throughout the collection, the authors were not particularly invited to make it their concern while preparing their submission. There were no precise indications from Black Fountain Press as to which theme the stories and poems should relate to. A vague working title, 'Status 2018', was the only indication given, with a word count in the case of prose. Rather than requesting submissions on themes like Luxembourg, or identity, the choice of genre and topic was deliberately left to the authors. This explains why some pieces are ostensibly set in Luxembourg or Ireland, Britain, the USA while others have no specific setting but embrace a kind of suggestive nowhere/everywhere environment. This is the case whenever authors place their focus on matters that require less of a geographic or sociological background. Biographical notices and, if they wished, answers to two questions – What does writing in English mean to you? Why do you write in English? – were requested at a later stage. They have been included at the end of the collection.

Statistics can be interesting for a project like this one. Of the 29 pieces included here, 4 are visibly set in Luxembourg, 1 in Ireland, 1 in Bangladesh, 1 in Ukraine, 1 in Britain, 1 in Germany, 1 in the USA, all the others remain opaque. The collection comprises 12 poems and 18 pieces of prose. Although we paid no attention to gender when we launched the call for submissions, we are pleased to notice that the anthology presents the work of 14 women and 15 men. With two women and one man on the board of editors, we seem to have reached a comfortable balance. The age range of our authors spans between 19 and 76, which means it is also representative of different generations of writers. We are aware that there are other authors out there in Luxembourg, who write in English, but who are not included in this collection. Regular followers of the literary scene will miss the names of Ariel Wagner-Parker or Anna Leader, to name but two. The collection does not claim to be exhaustive. In the process we discovered that the English literary landscape in Luxembourg is even richer than we were aware of. As far as nationalities are concerned, 8 countries are involved. 12 authors hold the Luxembourgish nationality, 2 have dual citizenship in the UK and Luxembourg, 2 in the USA and Luxembourg, 1 author holds dual citizenship in New Zealand and Ireland, 5 authors hold the British nationality, 3 the American nationality, 1 author is of Dutch nationality, 1 is Hungarian, 1 Bengali, 1 Irish.

What they all share is a home, the geographical home of Luxembourg or the linguistic home of English as a literary language. Above all, however, they share a love for writing, for stories, ideas, characters, plots, structure, rhythm and rhyme.

Pierre Joris

The Cormorant

is back,
one came as if called
— I did and I did not —
young, slightly hasty
movements, but an eager
steady beat like the best
drummer around, steady
line southward too,
just fifty yards off
shore & straight
down along it all the
way around the slight
bend at the 80th street
bridge, not so fast
young bird, I tried to
say to the cormorant as
I walked faster but re-
assured saw it's flight curve
& dip just as I reached
the bend, clearly landing
& I got there 2 minutes
later, scanned the surface
for my bird, couldn't see
the long neck, waited in
case it had gone under
to catch dinner, counted
the seconds to 136, but all
there was now was a

gaggle of ducks or
whatever you are supposed
to call 20 plus ducks
floating on the Narrows
Wednesday 10 January 2018
around 3:25 in the p.m.
& I didn't see the young
cormorant again, gone South,
probably belonged to the
Verrazano Bridge tribe whose
settlement was just a bit more
than 1/2 mile further along
— or maybe it was hiding
among the ducks like
Achilles was it among
the young girls and I no
Odysseus out to find or
to trick him out — no
ball to throw, no knees to
close or open — this here
& now is a different
world even though
sea & land here too
mix & link.

Cecile Somers

On Bridges Red

"Joséphine Charlotte," they said, "This is your bridge.
What colour would you like it?"
She pointed to her lipstick and said
"I like the colour red."

On good days it links the city with the K'Berg plateau,
on bad days it links life with death.

Perhaps painting it red was asking for trouble.

It was inaugurated in 1966
by men in black
suits
from what was then called the European Coal and Steel
Community.

How much steel does it take to build a bridge?

Soon the bridge became too hot to handle
for though it only lay there
like a quick red dachshund
that had lept over the lazy green Grund
the valley – now overshadowed by this big red beast –
called out the names of its pedestrians.

Some harked. And jumped.
Cursed by the inhabitants
living underneath the bridge

(how much wood does it take to build a new roof?)
the Luxembourg authorities
(who always like a spot in the top ten,
but not when it comes to EU suicide rates)
ordered a shield to be built.

Some quixotic architect designed a giant gerbil tunnel,
slashed it in half
and placed the sections on either side of the bridge.

It isn't the colour. It isn't the height.
It's the half-heartedness.
That will kill you every time.

- - - -

"Oh but no," the Grand-Duchess said,
"my lipstick wasn't quite so red;
it was more... gentle. Pink. Like salmon."

Of course they knew that, they had seen it –
but a salmony pink bridge? Le Pont *Saumon?*
That wouldn't have gone down well
(if you'll pardon the pun)

And what would the people have said?

It took a while but then they said it:
It isn't the colour, it isn't the height.
It's the half-heartedness will kill you every time.

Agnes Marton

Pink Benetton

Who am I to think I wouldn't stink
while shrugging away the chores,
even washing?

Busy with scrubbing the brand,
I swap crumbles for free seconds:
a cute, crunchy poet(ess),

fast treat for butler-served male chiefs
of the mind landscape.
On the flee

my luggage gets delayed,
the tracking number disappears.
There's a search

for a pink Benetton, hardshell,
four-wheeler. It was my home-
sweet-home, next of kin,

'second skin' plasters in it
for scar tissues. Gone.
I make a claim,

whenever I check, it says
'Whereabouts not known,
not yet.'

Around, spitfire mums nurse sons
they are forced to mute.
Pilgrims peep and pffft

at carousels till being told
to leave. The air-puffed bags they drag
plough the walkway.

I take the airport bus to town,
no coins for the fare; for once,
travelling light,

full of plans: shopping for
felt-tip pens, memory foam flips,
sea-flavoured toothpaste.

Terry Adams

Drive through Time

Drive east towards the border
Spring air, inch the window lower
Sunshine lightens winter's faded colours

Drive east towards the rivers, Moselle and Sûre
Drawn to water, refreshing, soothing, life giving
Think of my island home, rivers, powerful seas

Drive east, drive west, drive through memory's mist
Many Sunday afternoons we sought summer's water
No sea near but many lakes, rivers, ponds, streams

Drive along the flat Offaly roads, young children
clambering
Parents, deckchairs, sandwiches, newspapers, lemonade
treats
Dad at the wheel, the county map etched across his
features

Decamp near water: lake, river, pond, stream
Sometimes deep enough to swim in, if shallow
We'd seek pinkíns *, later explore empty rabbit burrows

Out to Bracknagh, or Mucklagh, or Durrow
Or towards the Slieve Bloom mountains, a bit further
The quiet farmer's bridge over the river near Clonaslee
Or on up to the Cathole Falls ringed by pure beauty

One place he would not go was the town pool
On a Sunday afternoon it was standing room full
In the thirties his Dad helped get it built
But he, disliking noise and crowds, avoided it

On my drive east I watch bare trees, savour memories
Anticipate the sights of the Moselle and the Sûre
And wonder how much of the present I would trade
For one bottle of P. and H. Egan's red lemonade

* pinkins: trout fry

Robert Schofield

To Start With

'It was a dark and stormy night and the two boys were lost in the forest. They weren't very scared because they had their magic friend with them. His name was Arthur.'

'You can't start like that,' he said and immediately regretted it. Harry, next to him on the sofa, looked up at him, and his large, brown eyes were round with hurt surprise and disappointment. Wanting him to retract, wanting comfort. He had his mother's eyes. Among many seductive aspects about her, her eyes too had seduced him. Projecting him as the source of comfort, before he realised, later, too soon, that he had become the object of disappointment. Perhaps always had been.

Rubbish. Her eyes had projected nothing. He had projected himself as being seduced (strange definition, to start with). Nowadays, he saw more clearly.

'Mummy said it was alright,' Harry said, still watching his father's face for a reaction. Mummy would.

Mummy was almost certainly too busy with her more recent husband and their family to spend time on textual analysis of Harry's school story project. Even just the beginning of it. And if she had found time, he couldn't help himself from thinking, she may not have noticed the infelicity anyway, let alone worried about it. Which, he also had to admit, reluctantly, would have been the better approach, all round. As it was, he had dismissed Harry's story before it had even begun and spread the disappointment across their precious, rare day together, like the rather moth-eaten tartan blanket across the back of the sofa. Once every other weekend, that was all the time they had together. Sometimes for the night, when he suspected they had packed the other children off to the husband's parents, conveniently nearby, and persuaded Harry to stay with his Daddy, so she and her husband could go out for dinner or whatever they did when 'free of the children.' Persuaded Harry. He thought he could tell, but of course never asked, just in case. So he fretted, and his fretting was the recurrent pattern in their days.

So much for a father's rights. Supposedly better than in many other countries, even embarrassingly so (for whom exactly?). Women got screwed in divorces, so they said, and men were allowed to do the screwing. Only in general, of course, but then he couldn't know, could he? It certainly wasn't the case in the particular.

It all hinged on Article 302, and the interest of the child. Which could change, he had argued, but without much conviction perhaps, whatever the embarrassing bias in favour of the general and the male. The tribunal would weigh up the greatest advantage of the child, as the Article required. A wide remit, this 'advantage', but eventually it just meant material advantage. And he was thoroughly outweighed.

He hadn't been well at the time of the divorce, of course, but he had recovered, and he was back in teaching now

Robert Schofield *To Start With*

because they needed decent English teachers at the International School. So all very stable, but outweighed nonetheless.

What about intellectual, spiritual advantage? Did it count for anything in the tribunal's rather brief deliberations? Could he now have another go, persuade the tribunal it was time to change the arrangement, as evidenced by the obvious imaginative inadequacy of his son's story written for school? Under the tutelage of his mother.

Even if Harry was against it? Even if he preferred the comfort and company of a home with a garden, and a new puppy, in Senningen. Equipped with one half-sister, also relatively new, a step-sister, and a step-dad with a large car. (Was the fact of his preference further evidence of his need to be... what?... rescued?) Weigh all that against a flat in town, rented on a teacher's salary. With olives and almonds sold in a little Spanish shop round the corner and, on a really still night during the festival, the sound of jazz rising like a cloud of midges out of the Grund. A bus and a stroll to the Museum of Natural History, or to listen to Palestrina in St Jean, or to Amy Macdonald next door at Abbey Neumünster. Not quite the space of the family home, to be fair, but still only ten minutes by train and a walk uphill to be out in the woods.

So quite possibly the best of both worlds.

He and Harry had spent a lot of time in the Gréngewald forest when he was married and living in what was then the family home. He would be up early in the morning at weekends, put Harry into the backpack contraption for toddlers and climb up to the plateau. There would hardly ever be anyone else about – perhaps a lone jogger or an off-road cyclist on the forest track – so he and Harry would listen for drumming woodpeckers, or wood warblers singing like one cent pieces on a glass table, spinning, coming to rest. Harry could catch the sounds out of the thickest, leaf-shaded air. Hares would lollop towards them, before working out what the tall, strange, double-headed shape was in the front corner of their eye, and then bash off the track into the verge. They'd come across the rootings of wild boar and, on one occasion, a family of them, three striped piglets in a line, a threat-eningly bristly adult at the front. Harry went rigid in the backpack, and so he retreated, gently, to let the pigs pass.

His wife used to sleep in.

You can't start like that. It's a cliché, commonplace, plat-itude. Whatever those words would mean for Harry. It was, he thought he recalled, the start of some Victorian or Edwardian brick-sized novel, unreadably overblown. He should look it up.

'Well. You want to start the story with something really interesting. And a dark and stormy night could be inter-esting,' he added hurriedly. 'But lots of people, I mean lots of writers, have used those words before, so they don't sound... very new. It's like wearing out your clothes.' He knew. As a boy, he had worn out all his jumpers at the elbow, and his mother was forever sewing on leather patches. You didn't see them on children nowadays, certainly not on his son. Banished by material advantage. Like chilblains.

'But I haven't ever seen it in a story, Daddy.' Harry, like the good boy he was, didn't want to be put off by vaguenesses. He was seeking a double approbation: come on, Daddy, just once, tell me you can agree with Mummy.

He was right, of course. Nobody would employ the phrase seriously. A cliché, almost by definition, could never be used. More fear of cliché than the cliché itself. Like a ghost. It's there because you say it's there.

'So it *was* a dark and stormy night, and there were two boys lost in the forest. They weren't very scared, because they had their magic friend with them. His name was Arthur.'

He read on, and Harry, seemingly happy enough not to have had an answer, snuggled in next to him. To keep him there, warm through the clean T-shirt Mummy had inevitably provided, he exaggerated the slow pace of his reading, ad-libbing, making detours, using the funny voices for each character (a tiny whisper for Arthur) that made Harry giggle. Harry knew he wouldn't be turning a page.

As he continued, at the door leading to the little front hallway where they could leave coats and muddy boots from the woods, a protruding splinter at the base of the door-frame (caused by a three-year-old former occupant on a tricycle ridden illicitly inside on the ancient parquet) began to tremble. Possibly in the faint movement of air from an open window. It was bulging somehow, and a tiny leaf appeared, ribbed and pale green like the inside of a lime. It shook in the breeze. A twig emerged from the splinter's crevice, and another at the joint between frame and skirting board. The faintest of rustlings as leaves unfolded and darkened while they grew. The door-frame was expanding as branchlets interwove, thickened and grew on further. Undergrowth formed.

Other branches began to obscure the door to the tiny balcony, and the lounge grew darker (in the agent's particulars, he had noted, bitterly, the little room was called the 'living'). He and Harry had their backs to the new trees and noticed nothing until the sofa began to sink into the soft leaf-mould at its feet. Alarmed, understandably, they scampered, both of them, under the table – though it was now more of a cave with luxurious growth spreading above it. The invisible and mostly inaudible Arthur came in behind. He seemed to be keeping all the branches at bay as they swung in the wind. There were trees, looming out of the night, and ghosts of trees, in the same way as the enormous willow at the foot of the Kirchberg hill shines beige in spring like a soul of its future self.

'Look, Dad,' Harry whispered. Stinging nettles were sprouting from the TV.

The two children were getting scared, after all, despite Arthur, because they could now hear the grunting and scruffling of wild boar coming down the track, even above the sound of the storm. They were probably, certainly, in

Robert Schofield *To Start With*

the boars' resting place in the cave under the thicket. The adults, with their piglets in tow, would be evil-tempered, and Harry and he, even Arthur, wouldn't be able to withstand a whole family of aggressive pigs. They were already barging at the table, furiously burping.

'Harry, I think we gotta go,' he said. 'You first.' He didn't want to lose sight of him in the tangle of roots. 'Quick.'

Harry set off at a rapid crawl. Hard to follow at his size, but he scrambled after him, a wayward bramble ripping at his arm. 'Wait,' he hissed, but Harry didn't appear to hear. They had paid no attention to Arthur, who was probably still in the cave. Left behind. Who knows if the boar could see through the trick of his invisibility. Perhaps his magic wouldn't protect him entirely from all those tusks and bristles and stamping trotters. He hesitated, but he couldn't go back. Harry was disappearing ahead. He daren't...

They reached the kitchenette, and he lay on the cool tiles, heaving a moment for breath. The balcony door was banging in the wind behind him. When he turned the light on, he saw Harry was filthy. Mud in his hair and smeared across his T-shirt. His own arm was bleeding slightly from the bramble. He ran his handkerchief under the tap and dabbed at the scratch, to make it sting.

What would Harry's mother say now? Nothing, perhaps. Nothing to him anyway. A tut at Harry and a comment that his father might have paid a bit of attention. Could have put him in one of his old T-shirts. And then she

Robert Schofield *To Start With*

would rehearse with her husband for the sake of the tribunal and Article 302 – how he'd barely looked after him during his allotted weekends. Came home soaked and caked in filth. More than boys' rough and tumble. He could hardly be trusted to care for him on just one day, and now talking of a more generous arrangement?

Or perhaps she wouldn't say any of it. Perhaps she would know she didn't need to. Particularly if Harry was still upset that Arthur didn't make it.

'I think he'll be alright, though,' he said. 'I'll check behind the sofa tomorrow.'

In the 'living', in the forest bent by the storm, it was still incredibly dark. Even so, Harry looked up at him as he was helping himself to a chocolate digestive from the open tin, and his wide, brown eyes smiled.

Jodie Dalgleish

The Day the River came in

She was glad when the river flooded because she was just so bored. She was bored with the way everything was always more of the same: past the post office and railway station along a concrete avenue, over the valley of an old town's fort, past the cobbled nesting of boutiques at which she would never shop. It seemed as if her bus number sat just behind her eyes while she waited for it to arrive. Her one-bedroom apartment tucked into rows of others, was unremarkable like the rise and fall of her breath.

When the river flooded, she drove out to the Moselle valley. She went to its most picturesque village – the one where perched plastic planters of multi-coloured petunias bring you into its narrow streets that pulse your wheels in a quivering of stone.

She drove in a flow of traffic down to the riverfront and its park, where the road was not even wide enough for two vehicles to pass. Like everyone else, she slowed to a crawl, through pooled water – up from the river and down from the spurt of hoses from houses: water into approaching water. Water fountained sideways out from under her car and splashed her windows. It slooshed up and over the push of her car's hood.

She swished slowly round the submerged main route and parked after the grey sprawl of water, along with all the others. She took photographs at the flood's edge, her coat done up to her throat. A small boy with his feet inside red plastic boots ventured in and did a little dance for his mother. A strange cyclist rode towards them, his feet and pedals underwater as he approached. The tops of road signs, park signs, buoys and a pontoon all lined the same aqueous plane, running from the river's brown raging torrent to the lapping at her feet. In the storm of the flow, rafts of split trunks and branches were being snagged by the tips of trees, boards and poles.

A fire truck arrived with flashing lights and pulled up not far from where they were. She took a photo as the uniformed young men stepped out onto the concrete berm. They were always at hand and people went over to talk. 'This is nothing,' she heard a man say from the enclosure of his jacket. 'This is nothing like it was before,' he said, pointing to the level of lintels and eaves. And she thought of herself stepping off the nearest roof into a boat, over its gunnels and onto a little wooden seat, a bag of warm clothes on her knees.

She wanted to see how far the river came, into the little streets. In her car, she opened the window and edged her way in and out of dead-ends. She was freewheeling a watery course as she leaned out and rolled and stopped. Here and there, people stood outside their houses looking at water, their doors left unshut.

At the end of the inmost rue, a couple was wading back and forth, moving contents out of their waterlogged base-ment, in a damp two-person human chain. Their water-proof pants were rolled up above the waves at their knees.

He went into the wet cave and came out with one thing after another. She took bottles of wine, kindling, tools, and stacked them into crates that she lugged up their steps. She came out with them empty, her hands dripping towards the next.

That night, back in her first floor apartment, when she lay in bed and closed her eyes, she saw water as if it came into her building's basement. Stretched out on her back, she felt laid over water. Water was somehow deep and cool, under her sleep. She was living suspended in a house of water. She was being overtaken by this new world, its fill. It approached as she had also loved its light calm; smooth shine inside and outside of her floors and cupboards and walls. She wondered, what was this river to her now? The river that brought her another promise like a slumbering wrap of peace, that the river will come in.

Jodie Dalgleish *The Day the River came in*

Georges Kieffer

A Bigger Splash

Mortimer checks his old Timex for the umpteenth time. Fucking hell! One more hour to go! Schoolchildren are the worst. What with them rushing wildly all over the place, chasing each other breathlessly, laughing hysterically like cub hyenas, trying to touch … No respect! Who could blame their ignorance? Not their teachers, lounging lazily in the downstairs coffee bar – *Partisserie* they call it, my arse! Talk about helicopter parents, working overtime, pay rise if the union is strong enough. Sipping their *latte macchiato,* or decaf double espresso, feng shui posh drinks, what the hell, I mean, what reason is there for them to complain? Wish I had a meagre crumble of their wages! Meanwhile their prodigal pupils create havoc, by setting off the alarm!

One more hour to go. Calm down. Tamax helps, and why am I talking to myself now? Belch, burp! And why take the money to the shrink, when booze boasts your ego and chases chaos? He can smell the drinks, the boss says, the alcohol vapours unvanquished by the minty layers of candy lozenges. I frigging hate my boss. And he hates me. But he cannot sack me, as I am permanently employed, so the document says, I am part of the exhibition, a person with special needs. Funny thing is, the driver was neither young nor drunk, but a seventy-year-old ditty who mistook the sidewalk for the road, drowsy, no glasses on, crash, boom, bang, hit me with her rusty Beetle and left me a casualty on the roadside. Thing is, can't even blame her, I mean, accidents are bound to happen any time …

Still. Yes, I do calm down, but it's not getting any better, not until I can see them on my own, not till I'm completely alone, yes, don't think I'm crazy, there's solace in working here! But they put me into this awful uniform, company policy, I look like a chimpanzee, hu, hu, hu, I make strange noises now and don't give a fart if anyone hears me, the place will be dead in a few minutes anyhow! As if these grey, oversized trousers and jacket could cover up my pain. Especially at night it's hellish: emptying the bottle, tossing my poor body from side to side, sweating, cars chasing me. I live alone in a shabby flat. Oh, but something I wanted to ask you, dear visitor, have you ever had an accident? How did you recover? Can you sleep at night? How long can you fight?

I've had enough, I say. Funny, how this place makes me nervous and soothes me at the same time. My Timex tells me three more minutes. Then I will have them for myself. And I will be the boss. Ha, just laugh, but let me tell you how it helps me. Yes, of late it has become really bad. The limp will stay forever. The uniform covers the sores, but does it take away the smells? Because I smell, that's what the big B keeps saying, I stink, hang him, I may be drinking way too much, or not, and I'll be washing in this pure, pristine (I stole this word from the wee card underneath the picture) water from the pond I'm just gazing at. On the fourth floor, which is where I work.

Yes, I keep talking to myself as there's no one bloody else to talk to! But I can watch the picture for hours and that's that. Silence. Soon it's closing time. It was different in hospital. Do you believe that: the old lady who ran me over came up to see me every single day. Her eyesight was bad, her hearing even worse. She brought me flowers, but you can't drink flowers, can you? Then assorted chocolates. I swallowed the sweet, creamy stuff filled with tiny drops of alcohol: Rum Saint James (1.73%), Rémy Martin Fine Champagne Cognac (1.63%), Cointreau (1.2%), Whisky Label 5 (1.68%). I had to have much more than that, oceans of booze. Poor lady, once she saw my needs she carried antique stocks of lethal Liebfraumilch to my hospital bed. Horrible taste, but I drowned it anyway. And Miss Winter sobbing, telling stories about her children never visiting, and then her old tomcat kicking the bucket!

She died last year, Miss Winter, please share a tiny thought for her. She made me a cripple, yes, but not on purpose. I glance at my watch. Visiting time's over. My time. There's a large window next to the painting, some fresh air gets in. From down the cobbled street filled with after-work frenzy and pre-drinking buzzing, people having fun, coming up to the fourth floor which is where I work, but I have told you that already, haven't I? The air is good, because it's hot in here, very hot, and it's only June. Soon I'll do the crazy thing, I guess it's tonight when I'll be joining them. The uniform is stupid, beyond description, so I won't do it, I mean, would you wear a silly hat? On top of that I get lousy wages, working hard for a living, that's why I will quit pretty soon, no damage done. I haven't told you yet what I do.

Georges Kieffer *A Bigger Splash*

Patient visitor, I am Mortimer, the museum attendant from the fourth floor, I say loudly but not proudly. It's a boring occupation, art connoisseurs are mostly rude or ignore me, dear colleagues don't give a cat's piss about me, it's testing my nerves by gosh, no wonder I'm getting pissed every night – what's your poison? – this job is sure tiring as hell, yes, they do allow me to sit on this seedy, second-hand joke of a chair, I'm an invalid after all, not fit for a regular, full-time job (before my accident I used to work as a lorry driver but that's another story and I won't torture you with that), yes, the insurance paid, a new life with old bones to take care of, fuck, it hurts, the fresh air fills my lungs, breathing, out in, out in, out in, ah, ah, it's getting a bit better but not much ...

I'm the boss now, alone at last. Funny how they close the gallery, never bothering to check all the floors for stray, strolling visitors. I even slept in the museum once, no one ever noticed. The bunkbed in the folklore section was very comfy. No folklore now. I'm the boss and reign supreme over them. God, how hot it is, I'm shaking and sweating like an animal in the zoo, I think I'll take off my clothes. I'm standing in front of them now, seeing every single detail, I'm lurking behind the tree, there are seven of them, lying lusciously in the grass, dreamily gazing at the pond. And who needs any arty-farty shit to describe the work, I mean, I've been toiling here for twelve fucking years, scratching my balls, and staring at this goddam painting!

Georges Kieffer *A Bigger Splash*

Jeff Schinker

The Soundtrack of their Lives

Nils Bore approached him after a gig. Will's band, The One-Eyed Snakes, a progressive post-rock band whose sense for creating dream-like atmospheres had been praised by several local fanzines, had achieved as much success as was to be expected within a musical genre whose biggest festival world-wide never attracted more than 5000 attendees. Which meant he had to consider it a huge success that a hundred fans were now drawn to the stage like hyenas to a rotten body, considering that neither he nor his fellow band members would ever be able to make a living from either their music, or the identically committed touring executed with as much time and passion.

Meanwhile, they had signed with a small German indie label that made sure their albums were available on every streaming service and in every one of the last world-wide CD and vinyl shops. Had gotten critical acclaim for their "revolutionary use of the fuzz pedal", had been qualified, after they had published their moody single "I'm Garlick, You're Vampire", as "David Lynch's worst nightmare", and, most flatteringly, had been compared to one of their biggest sources of inspiration, Transgender Amputee Chicks from Mars. Unfortunately, TACM were just going through a very harsh split from their drummer Kurt "The C(l)ock" Korona, who never showed up on time, be it for their rehearsals, their gigs or even their encores, which had led TACM to "discreetly, gradually" replace him with a drum-machine, without Kurt Korona even noticing he was being disposed of.

This was a constant topic of discussion and source of internal bickering, and it was while they were debating the dismissal of Korona for the umpteenth time that Will noticed, from the corner of his eye and through the haze of the venue – spits of smoke were exuding the old fog machine and Jerry, the band's sound engineer, was still experimenting with the lights, aimlessly going through various shades of blue, pink, and red as if he was looking for deep revelations or some hidden meaning at the heart of the colour spectrum – that someone was trying to get his attention.

Nils Bore introduced himself as a wealthy, retired banker – now in his early forties, he had made a lot of money and had been clever enough to comfortably hoard his income from the imploding economy on an offshore bank account. Once he had realized the Bacchanalian times of the 80s and 90s were coming to an end, he promptly ceased to speculate on a market he knew well enough to foresee its impending demise – well, to be honest, he told Will, his grin the embodiment of a man truly indifferent, he had carefully plotted its implosion and participated in the execution of the admittedly diabolical plan to blow up the economic bubble.

"But let's cut to the chase, we don't have much time, there's a maximum word count to this short story," Nils Bore went on, suddenly interrupting both his ramblings about his former life and the turn of indirect speech this story

Jeff Schinker *The Soundtrack of their Lives*

had taken, and to add further insult to injury, suddenly ending the common laws of plausibility he, as a regular fictional character, was supposed to abide by, thus making us suspend our disbelief – perhaps I shouldn't have called him Nils Bore to start with.

"I know all about your financial situation. About how you're trying to make ends meet and how it's not working out. How your little student jobs barely compensate for all the energy you so fruitlessly invest in making music. I'm here to offer you some help. A financial solution, a compromise, a new challenge."

Even though Will had no wife or children, he had none-theless begun to think think about getting an actual job. He had already set up lightshows and helped out behind giant mix tables at mainstream venues such as the "Tena-Plus-Venue" or the "Durex-Ultra-Thin-Arena" for several years now, that is when he wasn't pouring pints of ale, something he wasn't very good at, as there was always either too much froth or none at all, customers complaining about their beers because, due to one of these circumstances that made you curse life, as soon as he poured a beer with no froth on top, he'd hand it to a customer who liked to have a lot of foam on his Rosport Jaune and, conversely, whenever he drafted the beer so clumsily that the white and yellow layers of the pint glass were equally distrib-uted, he'd chance upon one of those Belgian or English customers who seemed to suffer from a froth allergy and promptly forced him to correct his mistake by adding more of the precious liquid, the queue, in the meantime, taking on frightening, almost nightmarish proportions.

For all of these reasons, he resisted the urge to dismiss Bore, mumbling something which Nils Bore interpreted quite rightly as an encouragement to keep explaining.

"I'd like to hire you – for a monthly fee worth ten times what you're making now ..."

"You have no idea how much I'm ..."

"Up to 900 euros, if you have a lot of shows. Don't interrupt me, it distracts me and I'm not used to that. I'd like to hire you to write the soundtrack of my life. Well, to be precise: to write the soundtrack to the lives my wife and I are leading. Consider it an honour. We both like what you're doing and we deem you worthy and sophisticated enough to devote your skills to such an ambitious, challenging, and, well, complicated task. We want you to accompany our lives, to put the necessary emphasis on certain moments, to discreetly overplay some others, to add some emotion to something we've come to consider a tad dry. There'll be no scenic limitations, no censorship, no barriers between us. When I make love to my wife, you'll have to sneak into our intimacy, to become my erect cock, to be her lust. Your crystalline notes must turn into our moist palms – your erotic crescendo won't follow ours, it must guide us, lead the way, trigger it. But I guess the most challenging part will be to spice up the dull parts of our lives – the morning routine of showering, the tediousness of going shopping, the boredom of cooking, the morose fitness sessions we attend to keep our bodies healthy, the dinners during which, after a long and happy but somehow glum marriage, there are John-Cageian moments of silence. There's a conucopia of words to express boredom in almost every language, don't you think? Up to you to strike the balance between emphasizing our apathy and giving us hope to escape it – art should always both mirror and transcend, right?"

–

Will knew he had no choice. For all the reasons mentioned above, and some others, and after a week-long fight with his inner self there's no time to develop here (we're not in some Russian 19th-century-novel), he sat down with his band members, explained how he was going to, for a year or so, devote himself to an avant-garde art project at the end of which he'd have assembled enough money to make them all live from their music and insisted that they should just keep touring with a substitute programmer and keyboarder (yes, I deliberately kept up the suspense, but now the cat is out of the bag, he plays the keys), adding that they shouldn't hold on to him – for Will would soon be back with renewed energy and money.

He then called Nils Bore and told him he was ready to start whatever day seemed appropriate, a few minutes after which a white limousine stopped in front of the apartment block where Will lived and a chauffeur, who looked as if he had been lifted straight from a film set, elegantly threw his few belongings in the trunk, extending his hand with a broad smile to introduce himself as Walt, Hi, I'm Walt, you'll have plenty of time to experiment with your new instruments on our way to the mansion. For indeed, there was a complete set of synthies, stage pianos, effect pedals and mixing tables in the back of the car. And so they drove off, as Will fastened his seatbelt in admiration of the set of instruments he had never dreamed of being able to own one day.

–

For the first few weeks, everything went well. Bore's wife, Andrea Bore-Insel, was charming in every way, and both she and her husband were big fans of Will's work, so that they were at moments exhilarated by what he came up with, bursting into applause every now and then as Will exploited his new material with a zeal that was as infectious as the dancy grooves that accompanied their first candle-light dinner. The subsequent excursion to their bedroom, something he had been afraid to do at first, turned out to be both pleasant and stimulating, although, after a while, while he was improvising on their playful scherzo of lust, he felt how he was strumming his way straight to the core of Andrea's desire. He sensed her gaze, lingering on him, which was soon joined by Bore's indecisive glances expressing both a thankfulness for seemingly restoring their libido as well as an undercurrent of jealousy. He felt an indistinct, indecipherable accusation pierce his heart while something else was throbbing against the seam of his trousers.

Will felt confused, unsure where this was supposed to be heading, but the next day, after a good night's sleep, he felt a flow of inspiration permeate him, and even though he had the impression it was the erotic tension that was co-composing whatever piece of music he wrote, the couple seemed to appreciate the result. Erotic bliss and happiness hung in the room like specks of dust. He inhaled it, became a part of this utopian setting – felt like the driving force behind it.

After a few weeks though, he felt a sudden change in the atmosphere – it was as though the inherent dullness that had seized the household before his arrival was slowly taking its toll, as if an ancient curse was making its presence known. When he entered the bedroom to play the most recent wake-up song he'd been composing through the night, Andrea Bore-Insel cast an indifferent gaze on him, an empty expression, as if her traits had been carved overnight into stone and as if it was this effigy he was now looking at, the original Andrea already long on her feet, showering or brewing three cups of coffee. But then the effigy moved, got up, went to take her shower and while he accompanied her to the bathroom, where another set of instruments had been installed at safe distance, taking his seat behind his extravagant Nord Stage 2, risking glances at her naked body, he couldn't help but notice the monotony of every rigid gesture she now accomplished, as if *rigor mortis* was already gnawing at her.

–

The following day, Bore introduced Jessica, a young woman who was sitting in the living room, sketching away at a notebook, who'd be in charge, from now on, Bore loudly and almost aggressively emphasized, with scripting their daily lives. They'd have to work together, she would go through every possible narrative situation and he'd have to double his efforts so as to avoid Andrea finding herself again in this state of utter dullness, and if they failed, well he hoped they remembered the contractual clauses and their consequences. Immediately after which, a quick glance at Jessica's facial expression confirmed Will's intuition that he wasn't the only one not to have read them at all, but who reads contracts nowadays. Has one of you ever read through the expansive ones a company like Apple makes you browse through at the end of their contract updates, and if you have, Will, Jessica and I'd have to pity you for the loss of time as well as envy you for avoiding the possible consequences they might have to face, the nature of which they were utterly unaware of.

For several weeks, this worked just fine, and after a night of too much wine, Jessica and Will inevitably ended up channeling their creative input into more concrete libidinal activities – observing Andrea Bore-Insel fucking Bore (who wasn't handsome, but she made up for it) almost every night had convinced them there was an erotic attraction between both of them as well, although they had no way of telling whether it was due to context or something more intrinsic, more organic (but maybe this kind of distinction was irrelevant anyway, Will thought).

After a few weeks, the team was joined by Peter Dull, most of whose movies Will had seen, as well as Lucie Blasée and Ringo Chiez, two actors who had once performed in a video clip The One-Eyed Snake had filmed. Bore yelled instructions, his face both flushed with anger and pale with anxiety. They now produced the most incredible of screenplays, plunged Nils and Andrea into luscious make-believe settings, alternative realities blossoming with complexity, phantasmagorical fictional scenarios that could have been Academy material: there were decors from science-fiction movies and Western movies, there were all kinds of orgies and wild, surreal costumes. Will was writing score to nerve-racking heists, tear-jerking alien movies, tedious soap and ridiculous space operas where the budgetary limitations seriously harmed the rendering of décor while Lucie and Ringo were taking turns in playing enemies and sidekicks. Andrea Bore-Insel was ecstatic, and everyone seemed to be bathing in bliss (everyone but you, dear reader, because you can tell we got one paragraph left, and you know how bad luck always gets its way).

–

After a few weeks though, Andrea Bore-Insel woke up with her now much feared marmoreal face and Bore disappeared in his office for several hours. When Ringo heard a cry of someone in agony, he expected the worst. Entering the master bedroom, he saw Will on top of Andrea, blood gushing from his throat. Jessica was holding the knife she had taken from Bore's helpless hands, talking in a plain voice, explaining how she had meant to break open their closed circuit, that this was the only solution, describing how she had told Will to touch Andrea's body as though it were the pad of some of his obscure electronic plays, and how this had struck some sweet spot, some very sweet and very wet spot inside of Bore-Insel, it was her fault, Jessica repeated, sobbing while Bore quietly asked everyone to leave the room, everyone except Jessica, he needed her to make up the next plot twist. And this is where I choose to insert our weekly cliff-hanger.

Claudine Muno

Stephen

On his first day of school, the boy told them that his name was Stephen. There was some confusion, initially, because the forms clearly stated that his real name must be Tom, but he pretended otherwise with such conviction that by the second week his friends and teachers could not remember why they might ever have doubted his word.

Tom had decided that Stephen would be the best possible boy. Stephen would be eloquent, where Tom was dull, Stephen would like to read where Tom's parents hardly ever picked up a book. In class he put up his hand more frequently than others because he liked to hear the teacher call his name. As he did not invite people to his house and always played out of his parents' earshot, it was a long time before his mother ever overheard someone use the name Stephen, but she imagined it to be a nickname or part of an elaborate game the boys had made up.

She was happy to see him surrounded by so many friends. At first she had feared that her son would appear to others as he appeared to her, quiet and unremarkable. Even after seven years, she could not say that she knew him very well. Was it because he did not let her see how he felt or because he felt nothing? It pained her a little bit to think that complete strangers had the privilege of getting to know a little boy who remained unknown to her. Why did he act so differently at home? She did not dare ask and comforted herself with the thought that perhaps she was the one who was privileged: with her he was able to be himself while he felt obliged to put up an act for everybody else.

But the boy did not act, he was in fact very careful never to tell a lie. Everything he claimed to be, he strived to become. He sometimes wondered whether it would be possible to gradually blend his identities together, but in the end he always decided against it. There could be no confusion and he never overstepped the line between both worlds because the difference was so easy to tell: Stephen was someone and accomplished things, whereas the other boy was no one and accomplished nothing.

Only his father sometimes looked at him with real disappointment. He much preferred the son he had always known, who was more like him and he was very sorry now to meet him only rarely, at breakfast or dinner, when the boy joined them at the table like a polite guest. His father's greatest fear was that he might not feel it if something ever happened to his son, like most parents say they do; he might not wake up at night and reach for the telephone. No, he would learn about it weeks or months later, the way he learned about most of what happened to Tom. The letters he wrote to them when he was away at university could as well be entirely made up. What difference did it make? His parents would never meet the friends whose names their son mentioned or get to know the places he said to have visited.

When his parents fell ill and could no longer get by on their own, the boy returned home. After his father died and his mother became forgetful, he decided to bring Stephen in to take care of her. He was much better at it, patient and gentle, where Tom would have been unable to find the right words to comfort her. And fortunately Stephen did not take it too hard, her suffering did not affect him personally. After all, he hardly knew her.

Jessica Becker

The Square

She opens her eyes to the slotted light projected above her head. Fifteen strips of cold white light from the street lamp outside the room filtered through the half-open blinds, geometrically breaking across the ceiling and the two walls that her mattress is pushed up against. Uneven where the blinds are creased. The veiny cracks in the wall lend an organic texture to the diagram of parallel lines of light against the wall. The complex surface is soothing in the dark.

She reaches out an arm to touch the crack that runs from ceiling to floor near the head of the bed. Her fingers digging into its crevices. Every time she wakes up she picks at the edge of it, instinctively now, deepening the cleft, flesh and keratin sticking to the walls of the room, filling its fissures.

The numbers on her phone say 2:40 AM. She stretches her limbs. One into each corner of the mattress. She makes a star. Back arching with the stutter of a stiff body becoming conscious. The delicious feeling of inserting herself into the chilliest reaches of the bed. She imagines putty, melted across the bed, body spread like tallow.

She casts her arm out sideways, trails her middle finger over the floorboards. Across the floor in an arc to the hole in the mattress's side. One finger goes inside, pushing past the foam insulation to the spring coil, tracing its hourglass shape. Her eyes closed as her fingers move up and down the coils, measuring the rhythm of her synapses firing.

She swings her legs over onto the floor, past the edge of the mattress, strips off the quilt, peels her body off the mattress. Her eyes adjusting to the dark now, her fingertips lingering on the overloved sheet that covers the mattress in fits and starts. She plants her feet on the cold floor. Muscle memory takes her to the window. Fingers spread open the blinds. She watches the stark electric glare below. The single street light illuminates only this room. From the room it divulges nothing but itself and the neighboring wooden pole that hosts a wild knot of cables extending out in all directions, creating a network of wires that run down the alley and across to her building and to the buildings next to hers and across the street. She imagines herself a bird, roosting on the nest of wires, nurturing the discharging of signals into the darkness around her.

Her feet clamp down on the uneven floorboards. Toes spread wide so each one has firm contact with the ground. Palms on either side of the window frame. She affixes herself to the room. This her favored hour, when the room is permeated with the night's glare, its darkness made palpable.

Outside, her skin tenses against the wind even though the air is warm. She walks for fourteen blocks, slow and steady along streets that are clamorous by day but taciturn in the early morning hours. Dissipating into the spaces between the projected glow of one street lamp and the next, weaving in and out of the spotlight. Dark to light to dark.

She reaches an open area, the sidewalk giving way to half a city block of open space. Concrete slabs for sitting and planting but no life here now, only the waste of the day scattered around, flushed into the outer corners by the wind, and the dull buzz of traffic diminishing behind her as she crosses into the square.

In the center the figure. It is all curves in sleek reflective metal. Her hands on it, palms eager for surface as she circles its sculpted contours, the ins and outs of it, the polished edges of its body, sturdy and cold. She presses her nose against it, her breath clouding its sheen and blurring the image of her face. Beyond the fog of her exhalations only the concrete around her and the twinkling web of lights from the street and the buildings around the square are mirrored back.

On the street side the statue has a dimpled cleft where it meets the ground. Making an alcove. She lowers herself slowly, hands and hips and elbows and shoulders sinking one by one to meet the gray tessellated bricks of the plaza. She tucks a bended arm under her head. Her body curling, spine and backs of thighs pressed against the metal, soldered to the structure. Her muscles loosen. Spots of light in front and around, streaks of light overhead, distorted in the convex form rising above her. The lull of the sweet bright expanse of the square, the hush of transit beyond.

Joanna Easter

5AM

You wake up in the cold pre-dawn, rub the tiredness from your eyes. A shower, scalding hot, would be nice. But the boiler is broken, and the water chills you as you scrub your skin, raw and red and clean. It'll get fixed soon, the landlord promised. That was three weeks ago. Your wet feet feel gritty on the tiles.

Back to the bedroom, where it is warmer. You towel yourself down. You put on your clothes. The same every day, in variations of grey and blue. A shirt, a jumper. Clean jeans. Socks that were once white, now dishwater grey. Nobody sees. Nobody minds. Your watch feels cold and metallic on the sensitive skin of your wrist, but your shoes – black and scuffed, fitted to your feet from years of use – are comfortable.

The kitchen is next. Bread from a plastic bag in the fridge. Two slices, toasted. Butter and marmalade, spread finely to the edges. Like every morning. It doesn't occur to you to mind. Instant coffee from the jar. It's quick and cheap. Efficient. What else could you want? What more? You look at your watch, no longer so cold thanks to your body heat. Heat, energy, blood flowing – these are part of you. These are you, but you forget. You are running two minutes late. You drink your coffee quickly, scald your mouth.

Your jacket is on the hook beside the door, just where you left it. Where you have left it every day for the past fifteen years, ever since you moved in. You put it on. It zips right up to your chin and the fleece lining, though no longer soft, keeps you warm enough. Your hat, too, is fleece. You are ready.

Out you go. Your rush does not prevent you from double-locking the door behind you. Then with a quick step you hurry towards the underground. The autumn mists rise around you, lending the city a ghostly allure – but it is lost on you. The subway sign looms, a bright beacon. You join the straggling band of devotees who walk towards it as though in a daze. The morning commute could be a communal experience, but it is not. Each person wraps their exhaustion around them like a shroud. Dozens – hundreds – of private little solitudes, all converging, never meeting.

But the mist contains other figures, too. They surge into view out of nowhere and reel crazily by. Sometimes alone, sometimes in twos and threes. Splashes of colour, bursts of laughter. Sharp and jarring to your early-morning sensibilities. These are the other denizens of this everyday dark. But their tunnel is ending, just as yours begins. These are the folks who have not slept at all. The mumblers, the stumblers, the royally screwed. And they laugh as you pass them by. *Fuck them all,* you think. To you, they are vomit-splashed abominations. Fumbling in dark alleyways, pissing against walls. You avert your eyes lest you see.

Your key is stiff in the lock, and your cold hands struggle to turn it. The shutters creak and squeal upwards, admonishing you for waking them at such an hour. The store is dark and empty. The bleach smell assaults your nostrils, but you can't shake the feeling that nothing is truly clean here. It never has been, not for as long as you have worked here. Twelve years, soon. They promised you a career, and here you are, assistant manager. You worked for this. You earned it. Those creatures outside, those young and restless beasts, they have never earned anything. Not like you have.

You turn the lights on, start the till. There's a puddle of something wet on the floor, and you sigh as you fetch a bucket and a cloth. Shipshape, shipshape. It seems like an impossible task sometimes. But you must set an example. You clean it up. Tidy some shelves. Time to open the doors.

The sun comes up slowly, struggling through the haze. Its weak cold light does nothing to alleviate the grey. It only emphasises it. No colour. No warmth. Your first customer comes in. Blonde hair, dark roots showing. Marlboro lights, please. She fishes around in her purse for the change, and as she hands it to you she leans in a little too close and you catch a whiff of last night on her breath. You hand her the cigarettes at arm's length, and she shuffles out, lighting up before she's quite out the door. You open your mouth to say something, but she's already gone.

Your team drips in one by one. Your team. Those are the words you're supposed to use, but they don't feel appropriate. After all, you do most of the work around here. Layabouts, the lot of them. They could learn a thing or two from you. You catch them laughing in the breakroom sometimes. You're almost certain that Kevin helps himself to chocolate bars when you're not looking, but you've never caught him in the act, though you would dearly like to.

Next come the morning regulars. Milk and bread rolls go through the till. Sometimes coffee or jam. Mumbled greetings, or none at all. One customer knows you by name and you look up in surprise, but he's leaving already, counting his change as he goes.

The elderly come in a little later, generally. One or two are early risers, but most of them go soft in retirement, never leaving home before ten. They like to haggle, not understanding that you do not set the prices. I'm sorry ma'am, there's nothing I can do. Most mutter acceptance, some mutter curses. But there's nothing you can do. You did not become assistant manager for nothing.

Cigarette breaks. Lunch breaks. All carefully regulated, timed. A stale sandwich from the fridge, paid for of course. Ham and cheese. The ham already curling at the edges, like salty pink cardboard. And then come the schoolchildren. Trying to crowd in, but you rap on the counter and point to the sign. *Only three schoolchildren allowed at any one time.* Their faces fall at the reprimand, and they throng back outside. You keep watching them, eyes eagle-sharp. Two of them have been loitering near the magazine rack, and you haven't been able to see exactly what they've been doing. Then you realise that children probably don't read magazines anymore, and feel a little relieved. One less thing to worry about.

The afternoon is long and dark. An old man knocks over a few bottles of wine with his walking stick. He apologises profusely, and knocks over two more bottles as he bends down to help you clean up the mess. You ask him to leave.

You take a five-minute break. There is an empty cake tin in the breakroom, remnants of icing smeared on the lid. You demand to know the meaning of this. Karen, blushing, tells you it is her birthday. Have a good one, you say. You're not exactly sure what you mean by that, but it's too late.

You watch the skies change back to grey, then to black. Time to go home. You put on your jacket, and zip it up to your chin. You put on your black fleece hat. And you step outside. Back into the dark.

And as you walk towards the subway sign, its brightness blinds you. The wind is biting, and it stings your face. And whether it is this or something else, you find yourself crying. You have become one with the city, you realise. You too are colourless. Grey and cold. Suddenly all you crave is warmth, and around the next corner you find it. Mellow light spilling into the street, and music. You go inside. Cautiously, cautiously. You feel like a wild animal, caught in the headlights. Drawn, yet repulsed. The heat hits you like a wall, and you feel your muscles relax. Here is a place you can stay for a while, you think.

And you are greeted with a friendly hail. It feels strange. You are asked what you would like, and you stare blankly. Then you say, surprise me. You have never wanted to be surprised before, and you wonder at yourself. The barman brings you something dark and strong, and though it burns your throat as you swallow, it feels like heaven. He catches the look on your face and smiles. Another? You nod.

You don't know how long you have sat there. At some point the large TV screen behind the bar comes on and shows a football game. The bar fills up, and soon there are crowds all around you, cheering and shouting. You have another drink, and find yourself joining it. You don't even know who you're cheering for, but you feel something. Something joyous that you had forgotten you were capable of. The fellow next to you is a lot younger – eighteen, nineteen maybe. But he throws an arm around your shoulder like a long-lost comrade. Big fan? He asks. And though you don't even know what you're pretending to be a fan of, you nod. He pats you on the back. *Another for my friend,* he tells the barman.

After the game ends, the crowd mills around for a while, celebrating what you suppose is some kind of victory. Then they trickle out. The barman wipes down the counter, and before you know it it's *last call, last call.* The bar is empty, empty apart from you and a dark-haired woman nursing a glass of wine. She acknowledges you with a nod, and you feel pleased. She knows the barman, and as you watch she wrangles a whole bottle of wine out of him. *To go,* she says. And just as you feel wistful that she is leaving, she tugs your sleeve. *Follow.* The message is clear.

And follow you do. Down to the river, where you take off you jacket, and you sit down side by side. The bottle goes back and forth, and you talk. About what? Afterwards your don't remember. She rolls a joint and passes it to you, and you accept. The lights seem blurry and bright, and you mouth is dry, and sticky like dough. You have some more wine. Then she tells you she has to go. You get up, and she gives you a hug, turns on her heel and leaves.

That's it. Nothing else happens. She's left you with the rest of the bottle, and you sip it slowly as you wander through the lightening streets. And from the mist, figures appear. Grey-jacketed, black-shoed figures, wrapped in shrouds of exhaustion. Stumbling and mumbling, royally screwed. But you? You're feeling young and restless, and as they eye you with disdain you laugh, and all you can think is *fuck them all.*

Tom Hengen

Memorable Journey:
The Family of Man revisited

I

The arms of the unborn
stretch out to grasp
nothing. Where chaos is
unquestioned, we are yet to be.
The umbilical chord modifies
the matrix. When it swings
lines are drawn.
Man starts wearing a mask.

II

The hunter hunts beasts.
The hunter hunts images
of himself – a masked man
is not without arms.
Killing is not
necessarily the opposite of
giving birth.

III

Now that the hunter can't help
hunting,
he enters a world where only the savage
survive.

IV The prey's grace colours the grass
   black in black, guts curl on the floor
   snake-like, trying to get back to life.
   The beaks of vultures could be smiling;
   one man's death. The vultures feed
   on grace. One man's death.
   Tribes and clans in the call of duty.
   One man's death.

V The jiving couple
   lost to the dance,
   much as the man
   to the gun at his head.
   All faces the same
   once they melt.

VI The woman screams.
   The baby chokes –
   screams.
   One man's death.
   The vulture circles and
   screams.
   One man's death.
   The mushroom sky devours all
   screams.

VII The little boy discovers
   a virgin flute.
   It emits sounds yet unheard,
   he walks it with stamina
   over the ruins of Hiroshima.

VIII   In a timeless ritual to shift souls,
         black and white mourners
         paving one man's final lap,
         howling mute sorrow
         wiped out before tomorrow.

IX   The eternal tenants ferrying
         the soul through the scenes.
         Cigarette burns on sunshine avenue,
         two toddlers hand in hand suspended
         in a tunnel of light,
         the divine simplicity of lady sublime,
         serenely staring
         and the horror ahead.

X   A dust cloud
                  is a dust cloud,
                is what our stories
                   are about.

XI   Snapshot of lovers embarked
         on an infinite yes
         in metropolitan bliss.
         Fragile shafts of light piercing
         the lightness of a swing in motion,
         secluded in the here and now,
         devoid of destruction,
         frozen still.

         A child laughs happily.

XII	Monochrome glimpses,
testimony to the fragile creature,
discharging red-eyed visitors
silently seeking within themselves
the strength to walk away.

Lambert Schlechter

Nine Lines

in the crevice of a Reovačka glacier
I come down upon the last king of Serbia

he shows me his toes, all black his nose,
all rotten, and his blown up eyes

this is such a bad encounter, Your Majesty
I say, and he says: you shouldn't have come

there was a time when we were happier he says,
and I say: let's get out of here, Your Majesty

but the crevice is too deep

for Charles Simic

Shehzar Doja

Inside the Haveli

It was dusk when we heard that voice
and entered the *Haveli* [1]. Then, there was only silence
between giggles and the rust
peeling from abstract tiles and the forgotten
arteries of ghosts were held by floating *diyas* [2] and the
soft light
pestered with insistence, fled and could not find its way
back again.

'Children are not allowed here at night' again and again
Our *ayya* [3] would insist, and that the light
seen with childlike amazement was to be forgotten,
tucked away in a solitary room to rust
like all of childhood before her. There was always to be
'silence'
locked in an anti-climactic battle in-between the
contempt of her voice.

It was something not easily forgotten, her voice
which would reverberate like the melancholic croak of
a frog somehow forgotten
by its army, yet, our disdain was marked by silence
upon decrypted walls and other innocent acts impervious
to rust.
It was in these moments that the resounding 'AGAIN?!'
would sound and we would cower away somewhere with
no light.

Breakfast was meticulously served after the
morning light
hit the corners of our eyes like ants under microscopes
and again
the melody of the *Azaan*[4] would float across and to
besides the old divan, a rust
coloured tapestry, completely insensate to sense from
where, a soft voice
would bring us, at least me, back to the forgotten
giddiness of the previous nights' dream in silence.

It would do good now to forget that embracing silence,
make my way back to the courtyard and search for the
voice
from so long ago. I do not know when I can again
find the ghosts hiding in the crevices of attics with
such delight.
I will try to discover when 'we' became just 'I', that
sporadic rust
that haunts the courtyard of our *haveli,* but not forgotten.

This is no place to be a forgotten
ghost, like the ones we used to catch till our *ayya's* voice
drowned us away from those *diyas* reflecting the
soft light
of the moon in glistening silence
and so we continue again
by repainting over the rust.

I have witnessed silence and the voice
we misconstrued for light and again,
it will not rust, nor be forgotten.

[1] Haveli: A generic term for a mansion in the Asian subcontinent. It is based on certain subcontinental architectural designs.

[2] Diyas: Oil Lamp made from clay that uses cotton wick dipped in vegetable oil or clarified butter

[3] Ayya: Maidservant. Akin to a nanny.

[4] Azaan: Muslim call to prayer. Heard from nearby mosque at least 5 times a day.

James Leader

A & E

When he saw her coming down the aisle,
In white, with the flowers in her hands,
His heart leapt up.
She blinked at him,
Dazzled by so much love,
By the enormous life that lay ahead,
As together they repeated 'I do' and 'I do,'
A lifetime ago.

Now, this February morning,
She's in a wheelchair,
And he's pushing her
Into the waiting room,
Slow, bent almost double.

Vicious what time has done to them,
How it's plucked off the hair
Till they're pink and raw as poultry,
Made her breathless and cranky,
Grumbling aloud,
Saying her heart's just fine
And why don't they leave her the hell alone.

Patient and mild, he waits out her squall,
Then answers for her:
Doctors, pills, dates, numbers.
He knows her heart,
Its history and rates and moods.

Nothing of them is the same, not a cell survives
Of the two strangers who promised,
With the crazy certainty of youth,
On that sunny afternoon,
And yet here they are.

All eyes have turned to them.
They stand, purged of their futures,
Raw and essential.
This is the point to which all our lives run,
And the question grows in the room:
When it's our turn,
Will we rise to it?

He stoops to whisper in her ear –
But they are her words, for her only,
She has earned them.

Her claw reaches for his,
The eyes soften into a smile
As she blinks at him,

And suddenly, they are beyond us,
Gone, taken wing.

Noëlle Manoni

Farewell

Limbs swaying, and yielding,
Made weak by age, and pain,
Lumbered, through the fencing,
On their ordinary lane.

The halter hanged unclosed,
On bony and frail cheeks,
And her ache and grieve dozed,
On Summer's last weeks.

Despite tenacity – Kronos took
As tribute the last untamed spark
And bewitched by his look
A proud athlete into a wreck!

With Winter a vanquished Amazon
Vanishes with the dust of decay
Into the peaceful world of shadows.

Robbie Martzen

Stargazing

She wanted more space
so he bought her a
telescope

in the hope of approaching asteroids
to dissolve the dark matter between
them.

They spent
skies full of night,
begrudging the waves
their dance with the
moon,

waiting for her eyeliner to drop
its heavy anchor
on dreamless shores.

Wendy Winn

Mandatory Birthday Hats

I kind of wish wearing birthday hats was mandatory,
like wearing seat belts when you drive.

I'd like a world where shiny pointy ridiculous
cardboard cones
could be spotted in traffic, at stores, at work …
bringing the person beneath it into focus, letting us
share their secret that today, on this very day,
they came into this world, wriggling and new like the rest
of us,
and if they were lucky, loved.

We'd notice them, we'd see them, we'd recognise
a human being, with a mother, at least, and a father too,
who had great, great grandparents who would have loved
to have seen them
in their pointy party hat,
who would have loved to have seen them … at all.

A human whose lineage stretches back past the Ice Age,
and who once learned to walk on wobbly legs
and learned the word for butterfly.

A human who rubs sleep out of their eyes and catches
their breath,
whose stomach rumbles and whose heart beats fast,
who is having a birthday in a life that is always short no
matter if it lasts for two years
or a hundred and twelve,
because birthdays, like all days,
are numbered.

And that's why we ought to notice.

The man in the car, the boy at the bus stop, the woman in
line ahead of you.
The little girl holding her father's hand, the man with a
crooked back.

People with plans, socks, hair, heartbreak,
kidneys, ticket stubs and cousins.

People who have birthdays. And who, I think, should
remind us.

Ruth Dugdall

Mother of the Groom

Marie Schmitt entered *Palais de Chine* and breathed in the comforting smell of battered oil, her ears soothed by the familiar tinkling chimes above the door of her favourite restaurant. Her old friend, Jian, was taking an order at a nearby table but he smiled over warmly at Marie, gesturing to her usual place at the corner table nearest the window. She removed her coat and slid into the red velvet seat, waiting for him to join her. From her clutch she took the envelope of photos that she had promised to bring with her.

She had much to tell him.

"Welcome home, Marie," Jian asked, "How was your trip?"

He placed the menu beside her though she knew it by heart. It was good food at the Palais, though not as good as when she had eaten the same dishes in China, seated beside her beloved son, Felix, listening to his stories of the country he had grown to love.

"It was wonderful," she said.
"Beautiful and very traditional."

When Felix left Luxembourg, four years ago, Marie knew nothing of the country. Now she could find her way around, even speak some of the language. What she loved most, though, were the traditions. The country was so steeped in culture; she appreciated the reverence shown to guests, the value placed on taking time with things. When she saw these values in China she remembered that things had been like that here too, the pace was slower and people had more time for courtesy. Or so she remembered from her girlhood.

She looked from the window, out to the Place d'Armes, where a bustle of bodies were making their home from work. Everyone seemed in a hurry, many were speaking importantly on their phones, pushing past, without acknowledging each other. But in China people saw her. Something about the slow pace of the rural community where Felix had made his home soothed her. Felix had been happy to pay for her to visit him, once for every year he had been there, and each time she had felt like she was stepping back into a world that respected age and traditions. And promises! Things Felix's father didn't understand, leaving Marie for his French mistress before Felix had learned to walk. She had felt disposable as a wife, now she was a mother, replaced by a newer model who was interested in things other than mushing up carrots and going to the park. That wouldn't happen in China, she was sure.

From then on it had been just her and Felix, and it was enough. When he took the job in China she'd felt bereft. Luxembourg seemed a different city without her son, emptier, and it was only her visits to him that had kept her buoyant, that happy month each year. Each time she visited she learned a little more of that wonderful country, and for the rest of the year she found solace here, in the *Palais de Chine,* where she could eat the food and close her eyes, and pretend she was with her son.

Jian touched her lightly on the hand. "It is good to see you, Marie. And I want to hear all about your trip. But first, I will get you some food. Number 52?"

She nodded, so glad that he understood what she needed without asking. She was desperately jet-lagged, and so very tired. But she didn't want to go home to her empty flat just yet. She wanted to be here with her friend, Jian, the only person who knew about her most recent trip.

Jian returned with steaming rice, and sticky pork, and fried broccoli. He placed the food in front of her and slid into the opposite seat, smiling as she began to eat. She hadn't realised just how hungry she was until the plum and sesame began its delicious magic in her mouth, and soon she had eaten most of the food. Happy, she sat back and pushed a small envelope across the table. "These are the photos of the wedding, Jian. You were right, the village is beautiful."

He looked surprised, one finger touched the envelope but did not open it. He looked around his restaurant, satisfied that none of his other guests were listening, then leaned forward and said in a whisper. "Please wait just one moment, Marie. I promise to return shortly."

When he returned he had a bottle of *crémant* and two glasses. He popped the cork, filled the flutes and passed one to her.

"To you, Marie," he toasted. "Mother of the groom. Now, please. Show me the pictures of my birthplace. I miss it so much, seeing it will make my heart sing."

Marie discreetly slid out the first photo, making sure that no one else had noticed what they were doing. It was a selfie, taken in the local hostel that was the nearest the village had to a hotel, given that not many tourists visited. She had captured a moment of excitement, when she was getting ready for the wedding, and her dark eyes had a glimmer.

"You are a very attractive woman, Marie," he said, formally. "And in this picture you look like a young woman whose life is about to begin."

"Hardly! I'm almost fifty!" Marie stifled a giggle, then realised the *crémant* had gone straight to her head. But Jian's compliment made her look at the picture with fresh eyes. Yes, she had looked good that morning. She had felt it too; for years she had dreamed of seeing her son married, and even when he reached the age of thirty he still hadn't met the right girl. Or boy. Marie was a modern woman, of democratic values and she simply wanted her son to be happy, but the truth was he had never shown much interest in having a relationship, he lived for his work.

Jian moved to the second picture, which was of the temple, simple yet beautiful. He put his hand to his chest. "Ah, I recall being a boy in this temple. All my aunts and uncles that I saw married here. I thought I might be married there myself, but here I am in Europe, a man approaching his fifth decade, with no bride."

Marie smiled sadly. "At least you haven't had to endure a divorce. I married too young, I think – I was only nineteen, just a child really. It had felt like I was playing dress-up, and no-one thought it would last. It turns out they were right." She pushed this thought away, wanting only to dwell on the good news she had come to share with her friend. "But Felix's wedding was so much more beautiful. Sombre, in a way, but it felt important. There was a *gravitas* that I have never seen at any wedding. And his marriage will last forever."

Marie reached for the photos and flicked through them, eager to show Jian a picture of Felix. Jian held the picture, frowning in concentration, then beamed at her.

"The bride's family are very fortunate to have him as a son. Such a handsome man."

Marie knew that Jian was being polite. Felix had been ill for eighteen months and the aggressive cancer had laid waste to his body. He had refused to let the disease beat him, refused also to return back to Luxembourg for treatment. She'd been sceptical about Chinese Medicine at first, but he had outlived the predictions of medical experts who had given him just six months to live. He had lived that extra year to the full.

Jian, as if reading Marie's thoughts, touched her hand with his own and kept it there. It felt warm and comforting.

"Felix looks so handsome, Marie. Just a touch pale, that is all."

She blinked away a sudden memory of kissing Felix's cheek. Carefully, so her lips didn't quite touch his skin, as she didn't want to have to re-do her lipstick or his own face make-up. But her son felt no nerves. It was Marie who was jittery, after all she had organised almost everything for the groom's side of the family. Felix's father hadn't been involved at all, he'd barely bothered with Felix since he walked out on them both, so she hadn't needed to involve him.

It wasn't easy, everyone else in the temple speaking a language she only knew a little. But she had resolved to enjoy herself, tasting each nibble that the waiters passed around, speaking to as many people as she could.

"It was all he ever wanted," Marie told Jian, speaking softly so no one else could hear. "Felix had been telling me for years, he just wanted to find a beautiful woman and get married. And he loved China, I knew he'd never marry a woman from here. But I didn't think it would really happen, he worked so hard he had no time for dating, and then he got so ill. Thank you for arranging everything, Jian." She laughed at what she had just said. "An arranged marriage! I never thought I'd do that for my son. Funny, isn't it?"

Jian said solemnly, "Arranged marriages rely on the knowledge of elders, and are a good basis for a union. But of course, love is what we all hope for."

He refilled her glass and together they toasted Felix and his bride. Marie felt giddy, probably the jet-lag made the alcohol affect her more acutely. And she did feel so very tired, but also happy and content.

"Now, you must have something sweet," Jian said. "I will return."

When he had gone Marie studied the final photo she had taken, the one of the actual ceremony. She closed her eyes, let herself return to the memory.

A gong had sounded, and a monk stepped forward, waving a bronze bowl of incense. Marie felt a flutter of excitement that the ceremony was about to begin, and stole just one kiss from the happy couple before she resumed her seat near the bride's family, some of whom were weeping.

She had taken her place next to the mother of the bride, and saw the woman's shoulders shaking with the effort of containing her tears. They may not share a common language but they were both saying goodbye to their children. Marie slid her hand into the woman's, they sat side by side and shoulder to shoulder as the ceremony commenced. Marie smiled at the woman at the point when Felix and his bride were officially declared as husband and wife. They must have both dreamed of this moment.

Jian returned, placing Marie's dessert on the table and also one for himself.

"If that is okay?" he asked.

"Of course it is."

It was nicer, to eat with someone else. Jian was the only other person who knew what had just happened in China, she had no one else to show her photos to. No one else would understand.

As he ate, Jian studied the picture of the bride's family.

"The Wongs are a very proper family, very respected in our village. Traditional and strong. An unmarried daughter brings terrible luck on a family, so when she passed into the other world without a groom there was much fear. It was simple good fortune that my own mother should tell me this, and that I knew of Felix's sad death, just a month before. It seemed like fate."

"You know, Jian, travelling to China to bury Felix was the worst thing I have ever done. But to return, just four weeks later, for his ghost wedding. Well," Marie was struggling to find the words, she felt so emotional. "It was a blessing. A closure, and a happy one."

This time it was Marie who placed her hand on Jian's, gently but also with some force.

"When I return to China next time, will you come with me?"

Jian smiled. He did not remove his hand, or his gaze.

"I would like that very much, Marie. We will go and visit Felix and his bride. Side by side, in the village cemetery.

And maybe we will go to the temple, together? There would be no sadness this time, and no crime either. Only what is traditional and right. I have waited a long time to return, and I want to go with you. If you will have me?"

Marie thought of the temple, the colours and the incense. She squeezed Jian's hand and smiled. They were bound together by the crime they had arranged, Felix's Ghost Wedding. Though traditional, it was also illegal, and yet it had been worth all the risk.

"I accept your proposal, Jian. Thank you."

For the first time since her son had died, Marie knew she had a future to look forward to.

Tullio Forgiarini

Daddy's Girl

Gerald Fischer dies today. He doesn't deserve it. Not at all.
He deserves to go on living forever. He's discovered pain
just recently and it would only be fair for him to suffer
a little longer. Much longer, in fact. But life isn't fair. So
Gerald Fischer will die at the age of 81, having suffered for
less than a year.

Gerald Fischer is what you commonly call a great man.
The number of obituaries you'll read in the papers over
the next days will be impressive. They'll come from the
grieving family. From his peers in the circles of finance
and industry. The world of the arts will deplore the loss of
a patron, charity organisations will mourn a great philan-
thropist. Several sports clubs will announce the depar-
ture of their long-time honorary president. Members of
Parliament will state they are deeply affected and so will
several ministers, maybe even the first in rank. As for the
Court... yes, I suppose even the Court will...

Of course, everybody knows that Gerald Fischer is a
monster. Everybody knows that he's destroyed dozens
of lives to reach the top. Thousands of lives actually, if
you count those who worked like slaves in the so-called
emerging nations. But they don't count. Gerald Fischer
built hospitals for them. And schools. And nurseries.
According to all, he did the best he could. But here, in
the civilised world, here, his attitude towards his friends
and associates seemed... reprehensible, to say the least.

That bastard! was a common addition to his name…
Disgust, yes, but often, very often, you could perceive
a touch of admiration; as if his ruthlessness were the
conditio sine qua non of his wealth and at the same time
the wealth of the small nation that will mourn him
tomorrow.

With his loved ones, his behaviour was even worse. His
beloved… A technical term, meaning his successive
wives, his mistresses and his only child. A girl. Me.

No, he didn't rape me. I suppose he would have done so, if
I had matched his predator-prey system. But I didn't.

Sex was always important to him. The breakfast of the
champions! And he is definitely a champion. He fucked
hundreds of women. Prostitutes mostly. He has a high
opinion of prostitutes. *They have a clear view of what's
happening and they don't hide behind ridiculous moral
smoke screens.* His quote. He has less consideration for his
mistresses. For the secretaries, psychologists, associates'
wives he fucked. They slept with him because he invited
them to fancy restaurants, took them to exotic places,
bought them gifts… *There is no cash, but it's still whoring,
hypocrisy included. Another of his quotes.*

His wives suffered the most. He had three of them. My
mother was the first. He drove her crazy. Intentionally.
Methodically. And to get rid of her he used me.

I was eight, nine. They fought a lot. At a certain point
he used to grab me and drag me into the car, telling my

mother he would drive the car into a tree. Very calmly. He would kill himself. And he would take me with him. He preferred to see his beloved daughter dead, rather than in the hands of a lunatic. A very sick person, that's what she was, my mom. And he pitied her for that!

We'd drive off, leaving my mother in tears, screaming. We'd go to a fast food restaurant. I liked that a lot. I always got the kid's menu. And an extra ice cream. I could play in the ball pit. Meanwhile, Gerald Fischer's phone would buzz incessantly. He'd check the number but not pick up. When he eventually did, it was always the police on the other end of the line. He pretended to be surprised at first, then alarmed, ultimately he would laugh out loud. He'd call me and I'd have to chat to the policewoman. Finally Fischer would apologise for his affected wife and flirt a bit with the woman.

After a couple of these expeditions, he got my mother drugged and put away. He divorced her without difficulty.

One of the last times I saw her, was at his wedding. His second wedding. She looked like a whale. A translucent whale. He had taken her out of the institution to show his open-mindedness and to finish her off.

I was twelve. I had to play a couple of tunes to show how well I did at music school. While I played *Wonderful tonight* on the electric guitar, he danced with his second wife. I remember his hands on her ass. Squeezing it. Mom died shortly afterwards and I got a horse.

Two years later, he sent me to a boarding school in Switzerland. I was allowed to take the horse with me. That kind of boarding school. With me, he spared no expenses. Never. I could ask for whatever I wanted. I did so for some time. I tested his limits and I discovered none. It took me two more years to understand. I stopped asking. I started to send back gifts. That made him nervous. I liked that. I sold the horse. I started cigarettes and weed. I was too afraid of alcohol and pills. My mom somehow saved my life at this time, I guess. I dyed my hair orange and had some unsatisfying sex with much older guys. Easy to understand why, even for a 17-year old. I didn't get a disease or a child.

I still took his money for studying: art, anthropology, psychology of course... I finished none of these studies. Didn't even come close to a bachelor. At the age of 23, I cut off the cash flow. I found a job in administration. Squalid and secure. I stayed away from men... I tried women, but didn't like it either. Since then, I fuck only in great necessity and utmost anonymity. Most of the time I masturbate.

I understand, he said. That was a lie. He didn't. He got angry. He could have crushed me. Like the others. I was aware of that. So I didn't burn all the bridges. I didn't go to see him, but I accepted dinner invitations, once a month. We went everywhere, from 3-star restaurants to kebab shops. He was always jolly. Subtly aggressive. I got used to it. It went on for years. He got older. *Milder,* I convinced myself. *Maybe I can win,* I thought.

Last year, in February, he cancelled our meeting. He called me to his bedside instead. I went, because I hoped he would die. I even delayed my visit for one day, hoping to see him dead.

They made me wait outside his bedroom. On a chair. *The nurse is still in,* they told me. It lasted quite a while. When she came out, we shook hands and had some meaningless chitchat. Her hand was clammy and her lips botoxed. I sniffed my hand, once she left. It smelled as I expected it would.

He was sitting in a hospital bed. He was wearing dark burgundy silk pyjamas. He smiled at me. *I have cancer,* he said. *I'm sorry,* I said. *No, you are not,* he said. I didn't say anything. He kept on smiling. *I am dying,* he said. I nodded. *But not immediately,* he added. *It can go on for a while. Months, they say. Even years… Yes?* I asked. Yes, he said. We fell silent. *I suffer,* he said eventually. *Quite a lot.* I nodded. *Do you like it?* he asked. *Seeing me suffer.* I nodded. He smiled. *I thought so,* he said. And: *I want you to kill me. Will you kill me?* He looked at me. His smile hadn't changed a bit. I waited to see if he would add *Please?* He didn't.

I got up and went for the door. *Will you come back?* he asked. I must have nodded.

I went back. Often. Once a week approximately. Some days, I hoped he would be dead when I arrived. But he wasn't. He was sitting there, with the very same grin on his face. The exact same grin he shows now. The grin of victory, as it occurred to me gradually. Pain means nothing to him. His pain, I mean. He got me back. Back in his net. I should never have come here. Or at least, I should never have come back. I realise now that he always knew he was winning. He knew that I came back to see him suffer. He knew that some days, I enjoyed it. And he knows now, that when I'm going to press the pillow on his face there may be mercy, but there will certainly be hate. And it won't erase the grin. It took him 50 years, but he got me. I'm definitely...

Sandra Schmit

Journey Home

Oh come on, man, move it. She drummed her fingers impatiently on the steering wheel. As soon as the mercury dropped below five, these people slowed down to a funeral pace. Like lizards. Needing heat to get anything done.

She just couldn't relate to that. Life was too short to take it easy. That's why god gave us speeding lanes. To sail past these bumbling pussyfoots, unless, of course, said pussy-feet decided to highjack her left lane. She mentally willed the driver in front to push down on the gas. Darling, this truck is barely making ninety, how long can it take you to pass it?

She snatched up her phone. Almost eight. The meeting had been endless. She really hoped Kas had gotten his ass up from the couch and started on the dinner. Not that he could be bothered lately. Since he had moved in with them, his oh-so-attractive power had morphed into a nerve-racking lethargy. From in action to inaction. Just like this guy in front of her. In the last ten seconds, he had barely advanced five picometers past the truck.

It must be something in the water, this decided lack of testosterone. She should have gone straight to the music school to pick up Tash. But then she would have had to sit around in the parking lot for half an hour, just wasting precious time. Besides, she had promised Kas to help with his tax return. And this diddly radio music was distinctly annoying. Why was everyone just so slow? She hit a button on the console. *Deees-pacito!* Hm. Much better.

Come to think of it, she could send him the word document that she had prepared to explain which expenses could be claimed by independents in Luxembourg. That way, he could already get started on it. Her hand grabbed towards the right. What had she done with her phone? With a sigh, she snatched her bag from the seat and rummaged through it. Where the hell... oh, there it was on the seat after all. Must have slipped under the bag. And the driver in front of her had just decided it was a nice idea to activate the right blinker. Sweet. He wanted to let her know that he was ready to free the lane for her. What a darling.

Shooshing him on his way, she opened whatsapp. While she was at it, better remind him of that promised stew, too.

"tax do tjis" she typed, and smiled. Kas hated it when she used her phone in the car. Too bad, couldn't be helped now. She hated the way he kept procrastinating on this, tonight they would get this done, come hell or high water. She selected the word file, added "amd food hungry" and hit enter. Done. Throwing the phone on the seat, she relaxed. She'd be home in half an hour.

Humming along to the song, both hands on the steering wheel and her focus one hundred percent back on the road, she banned all thoughts of to-do lists out of her head.

What was that idiot trying to... woh, tail lights, too close. She threw the steering around and her guts sloshed into her ribcage. Woaaahh... woaw. Fu--

Oh.

She took a deep breath. Slowly. In. Out. That felt ... good.

Phew. All easy. Straight road, smooth driving, no problem. Just don't look back and focus on the road ahead.

She laughed. A relieved, bubbly giggle, with a metallic taste of spittle rising up in her throat. Phew. *Quiero desnudarte a besos despacito.* She smiled. A wonderful warm feeling spread through her lap. Making love, slowly, sensuously, for hours. Suddenly, she longed for Kas' strong arms and his firm demanding hands. Wasn't that why they had moved in together in the first place? To have more time for lovemaking? Who cared about tax returns. If the government wanted money, they just had to come ask for it.

Firmo en las paredes de tu laberinto. This song seemed to be going on forever. Not that she minded. They should go on a holiday again. Making love in the sand all night long, looking up at the moon, the stars and, endlessly, into each other's eyes. The meaning of life, right there. Portugal. She'd never been to Portugal. Australia, yes, Brazil, sure, India, been there done that. But Portugal was right here at her doorstep, and yet she had never cared to visit. They say the Algarve is lovely in May. All the flowers in bloom. They would go and find out. Tash would be delighted to have the house to herself for a week. Life's too short.

She should message Tash, let her know that something had come up and that she needed to take the bus home. Then again, last week she had been at the school to pick up Tash, only to have her teenage daughter running past the car, in animated conversation with her friends, discussing cellos and boys and sprinting for the bus. She hadn't even seen her.

For a second, there was a deep, tight pain in her chest, like a metal shard piercing through her heart. Her baby didn't need her. But then the ache dissolved and made way for an airy breeze. She didn't need her anymore, they were both free to live, and love, and laugh. How wonderful was that?

She relaxed some more, gazing dreamily over the never-ending stretch of tarmac in front of her. An endless road to be explored. There was so much in the world to see and learn, instead of doing time in dreary business meetings. Deep down, she had always known that. Only yesterday, Dan had offered her a promotion and instead of jumping at her boss' neck in joy, she had promised to think about it. What was there to think about? A better job meant more hours to put in, more things to worry about. She would refuse the offer, and instead ask to work part time. And make that two weeks in Portugal, instead of one.

She had always wanted to learn how to sail. If she remembered well, Kas' parents owned a boat, back in his native Sweden. So her lovethrob probably knew his way around deck and could show her the ropes. Done deal: they'd rent a boat in Faro and sail down to Morocco. That would be such an adventure!

Is this the real life, is this just fantasy? She smiled. Spot on, Freddie, as always. She hadn't even noticed that *Despacito* had ended.

She couldn't help giggling. A big warm salty drop clouded her vision. So happy she could barely breathe. Life is good. Always. One hundred percent. Because the alternative sure isn't. So don't waste it all by worrying, especially not about other people's stuff. Because more often than not, they're not even that bothered about it themselves. *Open your eyes, look up to the sky.* The light you see took millions of years travelling the vast swathes of space, tiny photons determinedly speeding through the darkness, millennia upon millennia, so that after an eternity of nothingness, they can hurl themselves kamikaze style upon your retina, touching a nerve, proudly revealing to you the age-old beauty of their long lost home, just so that, for a second, you can feel happy and at peace. If that doesn't make you special, I don't know what will.

I'm just a poor girl, I need no sympathy. She raised her eyebrows. Oh. This wasn't Queen after all, this was Montserrat Caballé singing a requiem. Just as well. She listened and smiled, her eyes firmly on the road in front of her. All was good. There was still so much to explore. You know what they say: it ain't over …

Susan Alexander

Pequeño – A Brief History

Little hands.

The M&Ms were giggling. I looked my question.
"It's Pequeño," explained one of the Ms.
"Pequeño?"
"You know," said the other M. "Rick Reuss."
I knew Rick Reuss.
"Little hands, little feet, little…"
"Do you know that from experience?" I was curious.
"Eeuuw," said the Ms together.
"But that's what everyone says," said Missy.
"About little hands. That they mean he has a little thingy," added Merry.
"So that's why we're calling him Pequeño. It means little. In Spanish," Missy finished.
Merry and Missy – called the M&Ms by everyone in the Wall Street firm where we worked – were my assistants in the small marketing department that I managed. Both were blonde and girl-next-door pretty. Missy was sporty and ran marathons. Merry preferred baking brownies.
"He came in to see you and, when you weren't here, he started hitting on Missy," said Merry.
I considered. Rick was little. At 160 cm, we stood eye-to-eye. He had a stocky build, an over-sized, round head, thinning dark hair and sad, slightly protuberant dark eyes that reminded me of a Pug. He was our firm's leading institutional salesman and had not taken HR's

course on sexual harassment.

I sighed.

"I'll go find out what he wants."

"And you'll see that we're right," said Merry.

"Little hands, little feet, little..." they chorused.

"Stop!"

But I knew I was doomed.

A good idea at the time.

It turned out Rick had had an inspiration for a new business niche. As our company was a "boutique" investment bank and brokerage firm and encouraged internal entrepreneurship, I listened.

"Now that the Iron Curtain is down, there are lots of new millionaires in Eastern Europe with very few local investment products. I figure I could bring in a lot of business from there."

I nodded while I wondered what this had to do with me.

"But I'll need sales materials."

Ha. That explained it.

"We have the new corporate brochure," I suggested.

"In the native language. It shows commitment. That we're not just doing a hit-and-run."

"Slovakian?"

"Czech would be better. And Hungarian. And Russian, of course."

I should mention that this was the early 1990s and people were still astonished at how quickly the East had embraced capitalism. And that, while Rick's clients were usually pension funds and insurance companies, an individual who had an eight- or nine-figure net worth was also an interesting sales prospect.

"It won't be cheap."

"You've got a budget. I heard Hunt complaining about it the other day."

Hunt was Woodrow Forrestal Huntington IV, the head of Sales and my boss as well as Rick's. And you never called him "Woodrow" or "Woody." He was Mr Huntington until you were invited to call him "Hunt."

"I'll need his approval."

"I'll talk to Hunt. Get you on his agenda. And help you with your presentation."

At this point a warning alarm should have sounded. This was Rick's idea. Why should I do the presentation? But I had become distracted by what were indeed his little hands. And his little feet that were encased in expensive Italian designer loafers.

The M&Ms were right. Pequeño.

Left holding the bag.

Rick's brochures had been staggeringly expensive. Not only because of the translators' fees and the small print runs, but also because the lawyers had had to get involved to make sure we were not in violation of some local law. Most of my annual budget was gone and it was only July.

Still, the brochures looked good even if I couldn't tell the Czech from the Polish. I took a bunch and went down to show Rick. He was at his desk, putting things into a box.

"Moving?" As a top producer Rick rated a corner office rather than just a cubicle.

"No, I'm leaving. I got offered a $100,000 signing bonus and a higher commission payout. I couldn't refuse."

"But what about…" I indicated the brochures.

Rick shrugged. "Maybe the London office could use them."

I threw the brochures down on his desk and stalked off.

"What's her problem?" he muttered.

I was furious. But not as furious as Hunt. He called me into his office the next morning and waved some invoices at me.

"Have you gone crazy? Reuss is gone. Who's going to pay for all this?" he yelled.

Never apologize, never explain. I gritted my teeth.

Hunt's diatribe only stopped because the stock market opened. I returned to our office having been informed that I was not going to get any bonus that year and that the salary increases I had planned for the M&Ms were not going to happen either.

I was glad the girls were out. Then the phone rang. It was Claudia, an old college chum. She was the head of HR at a U.S. bank based in Luxembourg.

"Didn't you always tell me you wanted to live in Europe? Well, now's your chance. I've got a job for you. I expect you on the next plane."

As I rode in the taxi that was taking me to Newark Airport and my transatlantic flight, I thought of those boxes of brochures. In Czech. In Hungarian. In Polish. In Russian. I imagined them loaded onto a truck on its way to a nearby landfill. Along with Pequeño's dismembered body. It felt very Tony Soprano.

All the stereotypes are true.

A few years later I was back in New York to visit my parents. I was no longer at the bank, which never promoted women above middle management and had a pay gap wide enough to drive the proverbial truck through. I had launched my own marketing firm, with myself the sole employee, and was slowly building up a business.

Looking for possible clients, I had contacted my former Wall Street colleagues, including Rick. He had left the new firm, taken several years of bonuses and started his own hedge fund. Wall Street cowboys used to aspire to be rock stars. Now all they wanted were their very own hedge funds.

Rick was pleased to hear from me and invited me to see his new digs, a Park Avenue penthouse apartment with a terrace so big he claimed it needed a gardener. I was curious and agreed to meet for drinks.

Since I had last seen him, Rick had lost most of his hair and gained a lot of weight. He looked like a Colombian drug cartel chief you'd see on a TV show. Except I was sure "el Jefe" never whined about how badly his business was doing. How was he able to pay the gardener?

He was so self-absorbed and I was so bored that I failed to pay attention and ended up in bed with Pequeño, largely because it was an alternative to listening to him complain. I am omitting the details mainly because, after all this time, I really don't remember much. Except that the M&Ms were right. All the stereotypes are true.

A rose by any other name.

A few months later I got an email from a Heinrich Reuss. Heinrich? I knew a Richard Reuss. But it was indeed Pequeño.

"I want to see you. When are you back in the US?"

I ignored it.

Some months after that, I got another email. This was from Heinrich Reuss zu Greiz. Pequeño again.

"I have a surprise for you. Are you coming over for Christmas? Heinrich."

Ugh. I googled the new names. Reuss-Greiz was an old Germanic principality. And the princes of Reuss were always named Heinrich.

Oh dear. Rick was obviously spending too much time on ancestry.com. Either that or he had become delusional. I wondered what his clients thought. A rose by any other name was still Pequeño. And it was definitely TWFM – too weird for me.

Cyber-Weinstein.

From that point on, every few weeks I would get an email or FB message from Prince Pequeño.

"I had the most incredible dream about you. I want to tell you about it."

"I want to see you. Can I call you?"

"You can stay at my place when you come to the U.S."

"I've been fantasizing about you."

Then my mother was suddenly diagnosed with Stage 4 cancer. I left for New York immediately.

Pequeño found out where I was from a FB posting I made to alert family and friends.

"When can I see you?"

"Let me come pick you up. You can stay with me."

"I can cheer you up."

No "How is your mother?" No "How are you?" Just the innuendo. "I can cheer you up." And I finally understood that I did not exist as a real person for Pequeño. I was just a fantasy object he thought about while he played with his little thingy.

What goes around.

Missy and I had re-connected on Facebook. She had married Martin, who ran a successful hedge fund, and was living in Connecticut. They played squash, ran triathlons and spent two weeks helicopter skiing in the Canadian Rockies each year.

I got a PM from Missy on Messenger, along with a phone number.

"Hey. Thanks for calling. Remember Pequeño? Are you still in touch with him?"

It was more like he was still in touch with me.

"Um, kinda."

"He's asked Martin to make a big investment in this fund he runs. And used you as a reference."

"He did?"

"Yeah. So I wondered…"

I decided that brutal frankness was the way to go.

"Do you know the saying 'Too big to die, too small to live?' That's Rick's fund. He should have shut it down years ago. Taken his money out and retired to some beach. I wouldn't touch it with a barge pole."

"Okay, well, thanks. That's what Martin thinks too. But I wanted to check."

We reminisced. Merry was married, living in New Jersey with four kids. I imagined her brownies were sellouts at school bake sales. We agreed the three of us should meet for lunch in Manhattan the next time I was over.

La commedia è finita.

As for Pequeño, I heard that he'd had to give up his penthouse and move across the Hudson to cheaper digs in Hoboken. He continues to manage his fund, whose offices have decamped from Fifth Avenue to a less prestigious address on Lexington.

He also continues with the occasional email or FB message. On Valentine's Day. On my birthday. "I miss you."

So the question for me, I guess, is why I had not told Pequeño to sod off years ago. Why I had never confronted him about the consequences of his leaving me stuck with all those worthless brochures. And why I had ever, ever, under any circumstances, gone to bed with him.

And I decided, in reverse order, that as I have yet to feel guilty about any of the sex I had experienced, I am certainly not going to start feeling bad about bonking Pequeño. And as for the brochures, it is a case of *felix culpa.* While Rick had certainly left me to take the fall, the consequence had been my moving to Europe, where I have lived happily ever since.

I feel pity for the man. Pequeño is sad. Sad, sad, sad. It feels wrong to kick a man when he is down. Especially when I am so content. Plus I am curious to see just how long he will perseverate. I have always wanted to know the end of a story.

Jos Kayser

Cat's Jump

1. She was a young woman, quite tall, quite skinny.
    Her hair was ash blond, its colour had faded the night they
    killed her lover. Now she lived in that big western city she
    had fled to. The small flat was located on the 8th floor of a
    red brick complex with an inner patio. There was a single
    full-length window, half-protected by a grid. When Natalia
    opened the window, she was able to step out. An ashtray
    stood there and a bowl with milk for a tomcat that occa-
    sionally visited her. She didn't know its name, nor where it
    lived, but one day she had stood at the open window and
    had watched with amazement how he managed to jump
    from one ledge to another. Sometimes he even landed
    on the rail, before securing himself onto the sill. Most
    often he visited her in the early evening hours, just before
    Natalia left home to go out and dance.

2. Natalia came from Ukraine and she was a dancer.
    Not a professional dancer. It was her way to forget. When
    she danced, everything else faded away. At around ten
    in the evening, she put on her low-waist jeans and some
    very high heels. The thin straps of her tight top added
    some contour to a body otherwise composed of bones and
    skin. When she danced, everybody watched. Nobody ever
    approached her or made a move on her. After a few nights
    at the "Sunrise", entrance had become free of charge for
    her whenever she visited. People came to watch her. A lot
    of people, men and women, came to watch her. The way

she danced was captivating. She never paid for drinks. When the "Sunrise" closed in the early morning hours, she quickly changed her clothes and ran to the railway station, where she had to clean the public toilet.

3. Natalia came from Ukraine and she was a cleaning lady.
During the day, that's what she was. She was good at her job. The apron hid the dancer in her. But the way she cleaned also helped her to forget. She worked herself up into it, and the more she cleaned, the more intense it got. The regulars knew when she had finished and came to find an immaculate stall. When Natalia was on duty, more money found its way to the saucer. Sometimes, when she had almost finished her work, she slowed down. She wiped more slowly, took her time to wring the towel, and then, when she was alone in the changing room, overwhelmed by fatigue, almost imperceptible tears clouded her vision.

4. Natalia came from Ukraine and she was sad.
When she danced and when she worked, she forgot. When she was alone and awake, it was all there again. That night, her lover had gone to the meeting with the other men in town, the meeting that was supposed to be held secretly. Since their lips had separated, she had been anxious. She had implored him not to go, but he had insisted. If they wanted to save their town, they had to meet and decide on a strategy. An increasingly loud howling noise had torn apart the strange silence of that night, torn apart the barracks where the meeting was held, torn apart the men inside, torn apart her lover. Natalia hadn't run out of her house, she hadn't gone there like the other women.

5.   Natalia came from Ukraine and she was a widow even though she hadn't been married.

They had promised each other to get married, after all this, after the insanity of that war. After her cleaning job, she went home and tried to sleep. She didn't have a real bed – only a mattress on the floor and some sheets. No pillow. Natalia never really slept. She stayed in a state of observation. She watched the door as if she was waiting for it to open, for her lover to come in, wrap his arms around her and tell her how much he loved her. Natalia felt guilty when she woke up late in the evening, guilty that she had survived. She opened the window and lit a cigarette. When she saw the tomcat, she filled the bowl with fresh milk. He was black with yellow eyes. The last jump he had to deal with was from the opposite corner. Sensing the milk, he took the risk. He landed on the rail, slipped with his rear paws but elegantly saved himself from falling down. His tongue plunged into the milk, Natalia's hand made him purr. Natalia smiled.

6.   Natalia came from Ukraine and she was happy.

She put on lipstick and mascara, chose a short skirt for that evening's dance and a loose blouse showing the one or the other of her graceful shoulders as she moved. Once again, she danced. And they watched. They had come to watch Natalia dance. It was her night and the way she danced captivated the audience. There was nobody who could have disturbed her moves, invaded the invisible circle she had drawn around herself. Hundreds of spectators watched Natalia being alone.

7.   Natalia came from Ukraine and she was alone.
       Without ever having rejected anybody or consciously
       having given any signs, she had made it clear she didn't
       want to be approached. Men asked their partners to dance
       like Natalia, but they refused. Not out of jealousy, but for
       fear of being considered forgotten souls. No one ever came
       to ask her name after she stopped dancing.

8.   Natalia came from Ukraine and she had no name.
       But the tomcat had a name. Natalia shivered when she
       first heard a woman calling for him: "Dimitri!" It was her
       lover's name. She whispered 'Dimitri' to herself while she
       caressed the tomcat: 'Dimitri, is it you?' He quickly licked
       up some of the fresh milk and then jumped away from
       window to window until he disappeared into one of the
       flats. Natalia rubbed her eyes in disbelief. That night she
       danced a wild rhythm – she made strange, choppy moves
       and asked for cocktails all night long. The audience didn't
       realise, but she was different.

9.   Natalia came from Ukraine and she was different.
       When she came home in the early morning hours, she
       found Dimitri lying on the patio. At first she thought he
       was asleep, but when she caressed him, she discovered he
       was without life. A small trickle of blood ran out of the
       back of his head. 'Dimitri', she whispered affectionately.
       She left him there and went upstairs. She opened the
       window and looked down to see Dimitri lying there. Then
       she saw the broken bowl and understood.

10.   Natalia came from Ukraine and Dimitri was dead.
       She undid her high heels and took off all of her clothes.

The very last picture flashing through her mind was that of the empty grave back home, since they hadn't found any trace of her lover.

When she joined Dimitri, she had a smile on her face.

The officer thought she was lying there asleep beside the tomcat, but when he touched her hair, he discovered she was without life. A small trickle of blood ran out of the back of her head.

11. Natalia came from Ukraine and she was a poet. She held a few crumpled lines in her frail hand.

Dimitri, my love, I loved you,
Dimitri, my love, I lost you,
Dimitri, my love, I missed you,
Dimitri, my love, I mourned you,
Dimitri, my love, I found you,
Dimitri, my love, I'll join you.

Françoise Glod

By Train

My life has always been determined by trains. Every substantial moment of my existence was somehow linked to the railway. I was even born on a train. My mother, a stout, rosy-cheeked shopkeeper's daughter, didn't let her state of advanced pregnancy get in the way of paying her older sister a visit for her birthday. I wasn't supposed to come for another three weeks, so she wasn't going to change an old habit. However, I had other plans and signalled, as she told me later, by a couple of not very subtle foot kicks that I wanted to be released from my human prison. When I was older, I believed that it was the rocking movement of the train that made me want to crawl out of my mother's womb. The great turmoil induced by my mother's outcries had caused a crowd to gather, encircling her seat, staring curiously with open mouths at nature's strange timing. I guess people don't get to see amniotic fluid on the floor of a train very often and it caused a welcome change to the usual travelling adventures. Fortunately, one of the passengers turned out to be a nurse and soon after my mother's screams stopped, the train was filled with my first shrieks and people's congratulations. After having been the involuntary witness of one of God's everyday miracles, the spectators slowly dispersed and when we arrived at the next train station, an ambulance, called for on the radio by the train's conductor, awaited us.

At the hospital, the doctor suggested that, in order to honour the rather extraordinary circumstances under which my first contact with this world had taken place, I should be called Thomas, after Thomas Davenport, the American inventor of the electric motor, an invention that had made it possible to propel a small car around a circular track, which constituted the first recorded instance of an electric railway in 1835. My parents thanked the doctor for this insight and from then on I was known as Thomas Sternberg.

My fate was sealed and my lifelong obsession with trains and the railway was unleashed. As a child, I spent most of my time inside the house, lying on my stomach happily observing my little electric model railway and making choo-choo sounds until I was hoarse. My father had also presented me with a guard's cap and a shiny whistle, which I kept blowing incessantly, much to the annoyance of those around me. When the neighbourhood children were outside playing hide-and-seek and swapping marbles, I was in my room, imitating locomotive noises, screaming destinations, waving my arms in the air trying to be a living signal to the imaginary conductor and scolding the family cat for not being able to produce a valid ticket when asked.

My fascination with trains seemed immutable. Every time I took the train with my parents to visit a relative (not many people could afford cars back then), I was kneeling on the bench, pushing my nose against the cold resisting glass, producing the strangest shapes with my breath on the pane. I couldn't think of anything more perfect than the fields and trees and houses flashing by while my body was gently shaken by the clattering movement of the train gliding over the tracks.

I believed that the train was a fantastic giant snake, rattling its way through the natural wilderness and through the dangerous labyrinth of the city, never giving up its chase, only swiftly stopping to catch its breath before forever continuing its epic journey. I bombarded my fellow passengers with questions: How fast can it go? How many people can it bear? Will it go straight all the time? Where will the terminus be?

For me, the railway was one of the great wonders of the world, a fact that nobody apart from me and a handful of other aficionados seemed to appreciate. Like giant arms reaching out, rails uniting the country. If there was a river in the way, a bridge was constructed, if there was a mountain blocking the path, a tunnel was built. The railway was the ultimate means of communication, of bringing people together. Or so I thought. I wanted to study engineering to learn more about ferroequinology, but it was, of course, impossible for me to register at university.

It was also on a train where I encountered love, and I always considered meeting my wife as my second birth. It was shortly before we were banned from travelling on trains. Being smoothly swayed by the motion of the wagon, I looked around and like a sudden apparition, I perceived the most beautiful face I'd ever seen. Blinking a couple of times to make sure I hadn't fallen into a dazzling daydream, I realised that I was wide awake and that I had to do something. Although I suffered from chronic shyness, I couldn't resist this angelic face, girdled by thick soft brown curls. I got up and sat my trembling body down next to her.

The girl looked up from her book, smiled and said, *'Hello.'*

'Hello,' I replied.

'Are you a painter too, going to the conference on Surrealism?' she asked. *'I hope they will let us in,'* she added quietly.

And before I could even think about what she had said, I heard myself utter: *'Yes. I am. My name is Thomas.'*

We started talking to each other, but I do not recall anything from that conversation, all I remember is her face surrounded by those lush curls, her shining eyes and her melodious voice. When the train stopped in the town where the conference was held, the girl got up and grabbed her bag. I followed her and, in a daze, slowly descended the iron steps of the train. We spent all day together, exploring the little town, walking arm in arm through the narrow alleys that seemed to have emanated from a book on Medieval history, drawing us into a world long gone, waking in me the sensation that behind every corner would lurk the carriage of a nobleman drawn by four majestic white horses. We lost all feeling of time and place, but avoided the museum area after seeing grim-looking soldiers standing around the entrance, smoking and checking visitors. As it got colder and the sun was beginning to set, we realised how tired we were so we decided to start our return journey.

On the train, the girl took my hand into hers and said: *'You're not really a painter, are you?'*

'No. I'm just in love with you.'

'Just?' the girl asked with a smile on her face.

A year later we were married.

Many months went by before my wife and I were on the train together again. But this time, for the first time in my life, I was afraid of the journey. The giant snake, which I had considered until then to be a mystic hero, mighty and vigorous but well-disposed, now threatened to swallow me up whole and leave me undigested in its stomach until I suffocated. The train's vibration had become a death rattle. When I looked up I saw fear and horror in people's pale faces, dim eyes anxiously staring into the void, children wailing. There were no soft seats this time, no smiling ticket inspector to collect our fare or check our tickets and there was hardly any air to breathe. My wife was trying to reassure an older lady standing next to her, but after a while even her faint whispering died down and an awful silence took over, interrupted only by the train's slow and heavy motions jolting through the summer heat. The questions I had asked as a child came back to me: How many people are on the train? How many trains have gone this way before us? How many will come after? Where will the terminus be?

I was in the camp for six months, listening to the trains arriving every day. After the Russians came on a cold day in winter, we were put on a train again. This time, nobody had to stand up, no, everyone had his own seat although three of us would have fit onto one. Soldiers came and distributed lists with the names of the surviving victims from the women's camp. I concentrated on the cold silhouette of the naked light bulb, hanging from the wooden ceiling and quietly swaying in the air, just shedding enough light for me to read. While I was still frantically moving my index finger up and down the names I was asked to get out at the next station. When we arrived, the piece of paper was smudged with tears.

After life had gone back to normal, or what people accepted as normal back then, I started my engineering studies and finally became a railway engineer. What else could I possibly have become? My job concentrated on making plans, designing connections, I was responsible for the theoretical part of the railway system. I was the snake's head now. I could control where it was going, where it stopped, which rivers it crossed and which mountains it crawled under.

I never married again. I took up drawing in my free time and attended one or two evening courses in art history.

I am 96 years old now, a very old man. Today will be my last time on a train. I don't really like these new modern ones, their speed is so great that you get dizzy trying to look out of the window and their engines are so silent that you can almost hear your own breathing. A child is crying in one of the carriages up front. My beeper goes off. I should take my heart medicine every four hours, but I stopped taking it more than a week ago. I feel that I'll soon be at my destination. One last journey. The guard comes to check the tickets. Being a pensioner who worked for the railway company more than half his life, I show him my pass and he smiles at me, says *'Thank you, sir,'* and walks on.

I can feel the train slowly reducing its speed. I look out of the window and read the name on the sign on the train station: Oświęcim. I have arrived. Gladly I accept my neighbour's proffered elbow, heave myself out of the seat and stagger towards the automatic door. Standing on the platform, I look for a place to repose. Every step requires a great effort, but finally I manage to find a bench, sit down and try to catch my breath. Shuttle buses marked 'Auschwitz-Birkenau' are waiting for a noisy group of teenagers and their pale teacher who is frantically counting his students.

The train I have arrived in is still standing on the platform, then, with a shattering noise, the doors close. Somebody blows a whistle and a childhood vision returns. The train wriggles out of the station at a leisurely pace, slowly disappearing from sight. I look until there's only a minuscule black dot left against the horizon. Then it's gone. I close my eyes.

Jeffrey Palms

Wham! A Tram

People are throwing snowballs at me. I'm sitting on a park bench and an old lady who I thought was knitting was actually packing an ice-bomb which she lobs at me, fortunately at low velocity because she is pretty weak, being so old, but nevertheless it hits me square in the moustache. A pair of children slob poorly packed slushers at my knees and a handsome man of middle age fires a snowbullet at my sternum. A bird flies overhead and drops a snowman's severed head on me, bits of which trickle down my neck. The carrot-nose ends up piercing my arm and drawing blood.

'Christ,' I say.

Sophie sits next to me and people throw snowballs at her too, but she can catch them: some she tosses back, some she breaks open and nibbles on, some she discards, some she just lets pass by and fall to the ground. Sophie is a Luxembourger and she speaks every language that can be packed together here, and I am a foreigner and I mostly do not, which is why I'm the one getting pelted.

At the same time, I am alone with my thoughts, and luxuriate in the simplicity of being able to evaluate nothing but the snowballs themselves, as I see and feel them. This one's got some yellow snow, for example. I don't have to do a damn thing with them, and right there on the park bench I snooze off in the cold air, mid-bombardment, my ears numb and humming.

This is the general state of me every day when I ride the bus from Belair to Kierchbierg, where I work like a good Luxembourg expat. Words explode on me, I understand none of them, I moon blithely through my commute and take greedy, awful pleasure in that.

But today, the bus stops after the Rout Bréck and everyone pours out. This has never, ever happened.

'Christ,' I say.

I'm not at all the spontaneous type, nor am I blessed with a speedy mind. I'm more of a sit-and-thinker, chewing on thin slices of reality, the thinner the better. In other words, I don't get off the bus with the other 90% of the commuters, and I regret that while it's happening, but it's just not in my routine. The doors shut and I see everyone flooding across the street towards the shiny metal people machine, the tram, which I now understand began functioning this morning, and which is clean-cornered and colourful and Grand-Duke-approved.

'Christ!' I say, as the bus turns left – *not its usual route.*

I get off by the EIF building and walk back towards the tram in shame. I grumble widely about how nobody warned me, but the next day, gathering the energy to employ my pathetic French in deciphering a message on the bus screen, I notice for the first time a campaign alerting commuters that the routes will change on 10 December. I check my phone. Yup, 11 December.

Now I have no choice but to become a tram guy. The buses go off towards the EIF and disappear forever; who knows what routes they now take, they could well drop off a ledge into Hell for all I know. On my first tram homeward I sit next to a lanky gamer type, mid-twenties, who opens a Monster energy drink and eats two processed muffins (of a pack of four) that he unwraps from Auchan cellophane. Who eats on a brand-new tram? Who eats while commuting? I'm disgusted, I'm fascinated. On the next morning's tram, I see a lady reading: when her stop arrives, she puts her book into a clear plastic bag and then into her handbag. Extra protection from the rain. I get all fuzzy, watching her – I love watching careful people, especially if they're elderly. I become obsessed with the people on the tram. On Wednesday I see my colleague what's-her-face; on Friday, a guy in a cheap, ballooned suit; today, a lady visibly upset that the station jingles are being played *after* the tram has left the station that the jingle announces. I catch her glance and we roll our eyes together. I get it, lady, I get it. But secretly I dig that the jingles are messed up. It's like when people have crooked teeth.

Soon, the stories begin. My colleague Damien saw a girl trip over the tracks while the tram was bearing down on her. The tram driver blasted the horn and jammed on the brakes, gesticulating wildly. I guess 'the horn' was that recorded bell-chime, that nostalgic locomotive lullaby, unless there exists another, more alarming, alarm. She made it, but Damien concluded that she was an idiot.

'Christ,' I said.

Another colleague, Quentin, told me that the screens don't work, that they don't say the stops properly. 'They don't work,' he said. 'They don't say the stops properly.' I couldn't wait to verify his story on my way home. He was right!

Don't get me wrong: I'm madly at work on the local languages (except German – sorry Germans – I've got my mouth full with Luxembourgish and French). But there is a sleepy thrill in being smashed by snowballs. I knew a tram was in the works, but this morning, free of warning, *it's time.* You feel ultra-present – I mean, when you're picking ice-twigs out of your molars then you're definitely awake – but also ultra-pensive, very in touch with your mind as a private chamber of your own history, impressions, wills, wishes, and so on. Inside that head there's one little guy, your soul I guess, sitting in a room with tapestries from Dublin and Ann Arbor, listening to the blizzard outside the castle walls, reclining by the fireside with a glass of cognac and a book about the local environs. Sophie is there too, and she's actually been outside, which makes it so much more perfect. She says stuff like, 'They said on RTL today that someone drove straight into the side of the tram. The brand-new tram.'

'Christ,' I say.

Jean-Marc Lantz

Finn's Viewing

'I got up two hours before day
And I got a letter from my true love
I heard the blackbird and linnet say
That my love had crossed the ocean'

'Tá mo chleamhnas déanta (My match it is made)'
(Trad. arr. Morrison & Moloney)

- Don't get the Guinness, stranger! It may be good for you but Kilkenny's the better stout.
- That's what I told you at the dawn of time. Brewed by 'Wild Cats', eh?
- Don't go overboard on cultural references, it's not considered witty or cool in the countryside. You've been away from these Isles too long. Not everybody likes The Pogues up here anymore, they've always been more of a London thing. So ease up on the stereotypes, please.
- Difficult in such backward places. Nothing's changed, except for mobiles and more sports channels in pubs. Everyone's still dirt poor. I still see barefoot kids and mangy ponies outside ruins. Tower blocks slap bang on the moors. And they're still trying to tame the Travellers. This tiger's lost whatever stripes it had.
- Oh, come on, after all we're drinking in a converted church. How often do you get that in Donegal?
- Hate to disappoint you, mate! I had my last meal with Rosie in this very carvery. That was the Tour de France year. You could see the riders' names on the tarmac. Sorry,

not that different now.
- Well, it's going to get worse come 2019. There are enough knuckleheads on either side of the border waiting for the good ol' days. Forget the Good Friday Agreement. Doesn't bear thinking about. Just as well we're here now to enjoy it while it lasts, until all hell breaks loose again. Bloody Westminster fascists. I can see a catastrophe coming, no 'terrible beauty'.
- It's not just here, though, is it? It goes for the rest of the UK, too. If they go through with it, I ain't nevah comin' back, bruvver. Not even to London. Get out while you can! You could live with Millie's family in Esch.
- What about our kids? They were born here! And I still don't get your lingo. It'd be like you learning Welsh and Gaelic together! Great mix of accents just there, by the way. Let's talk about Rosie since we can't avoid it.
- God, that hair! It was the brightest of reds in the sunlight when she tossed it about in the wind. The pictures I took of her up on Bryn Pydin, behind your house! She wore it waist length, then. Admit it, those were the best of our Welsh days. Does she still have those awful green shirts for contrast? To emphasize she belongs to a dying breed?
- That's been proved bogus. Rumours spread by the hair-dye industry, but Rosie never trusted science. She hated it when I called her 'Chromosome 16'.
- I remember your terms of endearment, so sensitive and considerate. Or 'Freckles', like your cat. Really no surprise when … you know.
- Judging by her recent posts, there's a hint of grey in the O'Hanrahan mane nowadays, but she's as gorgeous as ever. Still letting her freak flag fly. Sad to say, I haven't seen her in ages. Sometimes I wonder …

- The Flaming Rose can never turn grey! I still don't get why were we invited. I mean, Belfast is close enough for you. But me? Did she really think I'd come all the way from bloody Luxembourg to attend the wake of her eejit of a husband? He wasn't 'maggot brain' for nothing. Was that because you mentioned me in your blog? Twenty years of silence, plus she knows I hated his guts. He wasn't even called Finn then, speaking of clichés. Pretentious git.
- Well, you did come, didn't you? And he simply felt he needed a more suitable name than Nigel 'Dickhead' Dickie for his work at the Abbey Theatre. When he was diagnosed, he'd just had a new Gaelic play commissioned, based on the Táin Bó Cúailnge, your favourite story. Rosie claims she's going to finish it. He did some truly great work. We co-wrote a radio play about Cú Chulainn and Dickie turned out to be a decent guy. I sent you the tape, in case you've conveniently forgotten. His parents despised all that Celtic Revival crap, but Finn went back to his roots. Literally speaking now, among the worms. It's a shame you never got to appreciate his talents. You're quite similar, actually, what with you learning how to spell your own language at last. Millie told me.
- That's different. He can watch his beloved shamrock grow from below now, can't he? Mind you, he's still above ground. I can't imagine staring at his corpse while getting pissed for three days in a row. Are we supposed to raise a toast to the stiff and chat with it? Is it an open casket viewing, like in the movies? Won't he start decomposing?
- The first day and night are only for prayer. Drinks will be served in the Spirit Grocery down the road. I managed to get a room upstairs. The actual wake lasts for two days until the burial. He won't get up, Rosie's had him embalmed.

Cost her a fortune. There'll be a kitty for contributions. Otherwise she may have to sell their cottage. No kids. Don't know what she's got planned for after the whole shebang.

- Funeral by crowdfunding? That's novel. I can't believe I toured the island with Mystery Woman after Uni. She wanted to show me her 'home'. Remember Kafka, my Beetle? That was his last hurrah. I left him at a scrap yard outside Dublin Airport. The end of an era. He'd broken down in every single town. On each mountain pass Rosie would place stones and the shells from her pilgrim's bag at the feet of the Virgin Mary to get a blessing for Kafka. We'd roll downhill out of gear and get stuck in the next hamlet. Then three weeks after I'd left I got 'the letter'.

- Once you go to England or beyond she drops you. You abandoned her for the safety of a steady job. I got the goodbye look when you two walked me to the station in Ceredigion. No warning signs. But there was Millie, of course. When I then left Luxembourg again to live in Belfast, I'd still broken the bond in her eyes. Millie'd taken over the regional Greenpeace office by then, so a return to Wales was out of the question and I was closer again. That's when I wrote 'The King of Yesterday'.

- Your best song by miles. But seriously, it had been on the cards for a while. There were 'issues'. I didn't know how to tell you. We didn't, actually.

- Issues. Let's not go through that again, shall we? So how was your trip?

- Well, I hired the car at Shannon, then Achill via Connemara. They don't hunt basking sharks there anymore. Sligo has the highest pavements in the world. I wonder how the old folks manage.

- An unfailing eye for the irrelevant detail, yet so blind to the big picture. So, tell me. What is this, ultimately? The Tour de Rosie? You went to Weebee Yeats' tower again, didn't you, you sentimental fool.
- Sláinte to you, too. Reptiles don't get nostalgic, do they? I found our names scratched into the parapet of Thoor Ballylee. We did that late in the afternoon one day when there were no visitors, like teenagers. They're still faintly visible. She'd spelt it 'Róisín'. I freshened them up with the same knife when nobody looked, scraping the lichen.
- Yuck! Were you like that with Millie, too? Rosie was never that icky when we were together. You bring out the mushy side in sensible people. No wonder she dumped you for Fionn mac Cumhaill, the self-styled Guardian of the Gaeltacht!
- He was such a phony, though. Fancy calling yourself McCool! It's hackneyed and so rural.
- Provincial. Let it rest, he's in Tír na nÓg. No real hell there. 'Eternally free and eternally young'.
- We said no quotes. Pint?
- Please. Did you finally get to see Slieve League?
- Nope. Three times lucky, I hope. I'll go back again. So much fog, us sightseers couldn't see the ends of our selfie-sticks. I went down to the same post office to buy the same postcard showing me what I was supposed to have seen. They've photoshopped the bracken and the heather. Shocking pinks and violets! That day, Rosie and I stayed up there shivering in Kafka for hours, waiting for the mist to dissolve. Not a chance. We were always happiest high up on clifftops. The car visibly rusted away from under our bums.
- An exquisite image. You and the rust-brown rose, lucky bastard. Are you still giving me that lift back to Belfast

after the viewing? You're catching your return flight from there, aren't you? Public transport's not so great and Millie needed the car. I'll chip in on the petrol.

- That's what we agreed upon, isn't it? Unless I decide to extend my hols. Maybe I can convince Rosie to accompany me to the cliffs one last time. The weather forecast is good. That cloud might lift yet.

- What cloud? Are you trying to get back in there? With him not even buried? Don't forget she summoned me too! And what about Dolores?

- Long story, forget it. I'll take you to Belfast, don't worry. I'd love to see the kids. And Mill. She's my childhood sweetheart, after all. But I never got to see Giant's Causeway because I stopped in Omagh Market Street with Rosie the day before the bombing. My first and only lamb mint sandwich! She wanted to leave the North immediately when it happened. Continuing our trip was useless. I think that's when she changed. She wasn't the same after that. We were on our way to protest against the Siege of Derry Parade. Finn had called upon everyone to sabotage the Orangemen. They were both Sinn Féin even then. She made me cross the border into Donegal and we stayed at The Rivering Waters. She was ashamed of her second thoughts and needed to rethink her position, she said. I guess Finn helped her to get her bearings back. I couldn't, I'd ridiculed her faith. I didn't know he'd followed her from Wales. It all ended here. Those were confusing days and I blew it. She might let me take her home this time. Or at least to the Causeway.

- Stop it! You've never told me that part. That side of hers wasn't so obvious at Uni. I simply never bothered with religion, especially in a Welsh town with as many chapels as pubs. Fifty-four at the time, weren't there? Was that the 'issue'? Colour me flabbergasted.

- Who's nostalgic now? Mary, the landlady at The Waters told us she'd fallen in love with a 'Derry man' at a country fair as a young colleen. A Protestant who came to see her clandestinely in the boot of a friend's car. He left Ulster and they got married. He'd died recently but you could feel she was still in love. She regularly went to Derry across the open border where she'd made 'new friends'. Mary was unbelievable, Rosie adored her like a long-lost Gran. It rebooted her belief in a unified country. Maybe that's why she stayed in the area. I've got a room there now, but Mary's long gone. Her daughter's running the place and she's getting on a bit, too. She's not as hopeful for the future as her mum was.

- It'll be interesting to hear Rosie's thoughts on the subject. She keeps shtum about politics in her posts. Good idea to meet here for a heads-up. You still a social media Neanderthal?

- I've evolved to Cro-Magnon, give me time. Is Rosie on Instagram? Speaking of prehistory, I almost had a religious experience today. I've just come from Grianan of Aileach, the ancient hillfort a mile from here. I drove up to Malin Head this morning, from where you can see Scotland. And now I could see all the way to Malin Head from the fort, it was amazing. I could even make out the mountain pass where I'd lit a candle for Finn and Rosie at the altar of the Virgin. There was only this young couple and me on the upper terrace of the ringfort facing the valleys and the hills beyond. The girl was heavily pregnant and her waters broke. When they'd left I was completely alone in the dusk. The Derry suburbs loomed in the distance. And then

I heard them: the drums. It was the Derry Parade again today! The beat of a marching army came to me from miles and miles through the air and I swear the pulse made the old stones tremble. I was a lonely outpost, guarding the fort. I was the one to bring my people the message: 'They are coming!' And I decided that I never ever wanted to live in a place where I'd hear those words one day: 'They are coming!'

- Shall we go to see Rosie?
- Yes, let's!

Jess Bauldry

Old Town

The first time I saw Old Town, I remember thinking how shiny and new it looked.

My dorm room friend, Jean, and I were standing on the crest of a hill. Forest gave way to a patchwork of fields and a kilometre ahead of us, cascading into a valley in the dry June heat was a settlement of white, modern-looking buildings. We had already cycled 40 kilometres from Jean's family's house in the Luxembourg wilderness, pedalling through creaky, rose-scented villages. We bound up steep, wooded roads, their sides speckled with wild strawberries, and emerged onto fields carpeted with golden corn. Then we freewheeled into the valleys, whooping like little kids, eager to be the first to reach the bottom. Until then we fed off our need to outdo one another. But, now I was tired and needed real fuel.

"Let's eat in Old Town," Jean suggested.

We were about to begin the descent when a smoky, open-top, khaki-coloured vehicle sped around the corner and down the hill. I glimpsed a man in the passenger seat dressed in a white robe. He had a long white beard. "Did you see that?" I asked.

Jean was already pursuing the smoky trail left by the Jeep. I followed as fast as I could, the wind roaring in my ears so loudly that I did not hear the music until we arrived at a security cabin. Jean flashed his ID card. "It's a secure town. It's for your safety as much as theirs," Jean said.

I handed over my passport. The guard took his time scanning it so when he gave it back I had to run to reach Jean. I found him at the end of an alley in a sunlit boulevard. He was surrounded by hundreds of old people waving at a convoy of military vehicles. It was like an old pensioners' Disney parade. Then the crowd cheered and I looked up to see the Jeep carrying the bearded, white-clad man.

He was tossing what looked like stones to the crowds. They fawned over the scattered gifts like chickens scrapping over grain. Some of the booty landed at my feet. I bent down to examine one and discovered it was a boiled sweet.

"Isn't it a bit early for Saint Nicolas?" I nudged Jean.

He shook his head. "In Old Town, Saint Nic visits every day."

"Eric? I knew it was you!" said a white-haired woman in a tracksuit as she approached us. She wrapped her wiry arms around my waist, enveloping me in a cloud of perfume.

"I'm not…" I spluttered.

"Eric, you missed Saint Nicolas, but I got you some sweets," the woman said, cupping her breasts and laughing.

Just then a bald man pulled up in a mobility scooter beside the woman. We hurried away as she turned to speak to him.

My stomach growled, reminding me why we had come to Old Town. The street was a pastiche of the kind of towns you might see in old photos: a pharmacy, several hair-dressers and there, on the corner, was what looked like a restaurant with a large yellow "M" hung over the door.

Automatic doors opened onto the fast food joint where a young woman welcomed us to McDonald's. "You're kidding me? Didn't McDonald's shut down 50 years ago?"

Over our burgers, I quizzed my friend. "What's the deal here? A theme park? Crazy experiment?"

"It's a dementia facility. Dementia sufferers are often stuck in a timewarp. Old Town is adapted to their reality."

"And this works?" I asked.

"Look around. Everyone is happy and they have their dignity."

We finished our burgers and the waitress who served us sat down next to Jean. "Aren't you a bit young for Old Town? Wait a minute, are you actually 80 but you found the elixir of youth?" I asked.

She looked nervously at me then spoke to Jean in a French too rapid for me to follow. I looked at the table next to ours, where a woman was making baby noises into a pram. A man was shouting in French to no one in particular while another woman was singing in English. After a few minutes Jean kissed the waitress on both cheeks and carried his rubbish to a bin.

"You two are getting on well."

"It's not like that," Jean said.

We passed through the automatic doors to bright sunshine where nothing remained of the parade but a few sweets. "Oh, shit!" I heard Jean say. I looked to the empty space beside the window where we had left our bikes.

"I think I know where they are," Jean said and bounded ahead of me. I followed him into a green shop named "Drucker's cycles".

A man with a bent back and upright shock of white hair stood behind the counter.

"Bonjour Paul. Nous voudrions acheter deux vélos," Jean explained.

The man nodded and shuffled to the back of the store, returning with our bikes, one missing its chain and the other the front wheel.

"Combien?" Jean asked.

The man scribbled something onto a scrap of paper and handed it to Jean. My friend raised an eyebrow, nodded and shook the man's hand. "Dans une heure, d'accord?"

"What are you doing, Jean? We're not paying this man for stealing and mutilating our bikes?"

"Relax, it won't cost us." Jean said. He passed me the piece of paper on which the old man had drawn a smiley face.

We toured Old Town, its smattering of shops and many hairdressers. Some were run by patients who, like Paul, played shop. Others were run by paid staff to ensure people were properly fed and cared for, Jean explained. In a leafy park beside a fountain, a group of women were playing chess. A man walked by tugging a yappy dog.

"How many times have you been here?" I asked. "Too many," he replied.

"You worked here?"

He nodded. I found it hard to believe, after all the stories we had shared while living in a dorm room during our first year at university, he had failed to tell me about this chapter of his life.

We both looked up to see we had arrived at a cinema. It was showing an old movie about a teenager and a scientist who time travel. We passed through the turnstiles and sat at the front. The film was difficult to hear over the circus in the screening room. A spritely man with a long beard was throwing popcorn at people around him and repeating things the actors said in the film. After 15 minutes, Jean and I gave up and returned to the street.

"What do you think of Old Town?" Jean asked.

"I feel like an explorer who has discovered a lost tribe. I don't know why you felt you had to keep it secret."

"It's kind of a discreet project. There are some people who don't agree with what they do here."

We walked on for 10 minutes, struggled up a steep hill and turned a corner to see a low, flat building next to a chimney. Beyond it was nobbly woodland. We had reached the edge of the town.

"Power station?" I asked.

"Nope. Crematorium. And there, in the forest, is a natural burial ground," said Jean.

"Oh!"

Somehow this explanation winded me more than the steep climb. Up on the hill, it felt as though I had left the strange dream world of Old Town. We looked down into the valley where people milled like white-haired ants. I thought of my own grandmother, whose photo I carried in my wallet. She lived out her final months in a sad hospital. Everyone said she had had a good death, but I wasn't convinced. Living out one's last years in Old Town, that was a good death. These people were really living at a time when everyone expected you to be passing away invisibly in some anonymous ward.

A sharp pain shot through my knees as we descended. I slowed to a standstill just as a siren filled the valley. A man came out of a modern squat building and beckoned us inside. He chatted to Jean.

"There's been an escape," Jean explained.

We followed the man into the building, entered a lift, plunged several floors and then walked along an empty corridor. We reached a large hall with platforms on different levels and a wall where a screen showed footage filmed from a drone. In it a man with a white shock of hair was riding a bike at an impressive pace along a country road.

"Drucker has gone awol," Jean said.

The footage then showed a security car driving behind the cyclist. Part of me wanted the poor bugger to get away even if it was safer for all concerned for him to return to Old Town. Just then the old man veered off the road into woodland. The drone rose over the lush tree canopy. Drucker was out of sight.

I should have known something was up then. But I was more preoccupied with the fact Drucker had made his escape on one of our bikes.

"I guess we'll have to ring your parents to give us a lift home," I said.

Jean shook his head. "We'll have to answer some questions first, like how he got hold of the bike."

I waited in the big hall for an hour until I was called in. A man questioned me in good English and my responses were filmed. It was late by the time we finished.

"You look tired," Jean greeted me in the corridor.

"Please tell me your parents are here" I said.

"I can't reach them. But, we can stay the night here in one of the staff studios," Jean replied.

I was too tired to argue so followed him down more corridors and into a lift. The door opened on a modern, tastefully furnished apartment. There was even a pair of pyjamas laid out on the bed in my size.

"This is staff quarters? I gotta get a job here," I said.

We ordered take-out pizza and watched cable TV until I dozed off in the double bed leaving the sofa to Jean.

I awoke the following morning to the sound of bird-song and the scent of coffee. My muscles ached as I climbed out of bed. I went into the living room. Jean was gone.

On the coffee table was a French press, a croissant and half a grapefruit. Beside it was my wallet. Where the hell was Jean? Just then the television lit up.

"Good morning, Eric," Jean said from the screen. The camera panned out to show a young man Jean's age, and an older, middle-aged man.

"Did they catch Drucker? Where are you, Jean?" My friend seemed not to hear me.

"I have to go home now," he said.

"OK, give me a minute," I replied.

"You don't understand, Eric." That name again. Eric. "This is your home."

Static filled the air.

"What are you talking about? I live in the US. We're roommates."

"No, Eric. I share a room with your grandson, Robert." The younger man waved on cue.

"Is this a joke?" I bounded for the front door handle. It was locked.

"I'm sorry we tricked you. It was the only way to get you to come back to the facility, willingly," Jean said.

I hammered on the door. "Can anyone hear me. Let me out. I am being held against my…"

"Dad, we've been through this before. After mum, we wanted you to have the best," the older man spoke this time.

I stared at the screen then grabbed my wallet, opening it to the photo of the old woman.

"That's mum, your wife," the same man said.

"No!" I said and switched off the screen. The dark black sheen reflected features I did not recognise: white hair, a deeply lined forehead and hooded eyes.

Catherine Bennett

The Elephant is out of the Basket

What's this, the elephant is out of the basket. How big was the basket? Why was the elephant in the basket? Who put it in there? And how did it get out?

Context.

We need context. We need more words.

What words do we need?

Well maybe add 'shopping' that would help. So the elephant is out of the shopping basket. That would create a scene wouldn't it? That we could work with. A lady walking around a shop with a shopping basket and putting items on the counter for the seller to scan a barcode. So maybe the shop assistant had scanned some other items and the lady asked, 'What about the elephant?'. In which case the shop assistant might say, 'ah, the elephant is out of the basket......it's already in the bag.'

Hhhhmmm yes that would work. So we would be talking about a little ornamental elephant, like those coloured ones they sell in gift shops and you can get small ones, or sometimes they have huge ones around the city or in people's gardens. Like they used to have those coloured cows. Yes, ghastly, aren't they, but clearly popular. No accounting for taste is there?

But what about if we added a different word?

Such as?

Like the elephant is released from the basket. So using the passive tense and now we are looking at a live being. We are looking at a proper elephant. The trouble is that it is quite incongruous, the idea of a basket caging an elephant. I mean actually that verb is there for a reason. Caging. We would need a cage for an elephant.

So what being would a basket be used for then?

A cat, a snake, oysters, just not an elephant. It would be pointless, wouldn't it? I mean it would not be strong enough to contain it. The elephant could roll it over. No, a basket would make no sense in his context. We need to think again. At the moment the shopping scenario has my vote.

What if it is a metaphor? Like 'the cat is out of the bag.'

What does that even mean?

It means that a secret has been let out?

Let out? Don't you mean someone has revealed a secret? Come clean as it were?

No, there is a subtle difference. The metaphor uses a cat thrashing around in a bag. We kind of know that the bag will not be able to contain this thrashing, clawing cat forever. At some stage the cat is going to get out. So the meaning signifies that someone (an individual) or some institution has attempted to hide a secret, but that it is so big it is bound to come out at some stage. The bag is not designed to contain the cat forever. It is just a matter of time. Do you see?

Yes, but then are we not back to the elephant and the basket? The metaphor would work for that very well. The basket is not capable of holding the elephant in for any length of time. So it will break out.

But hang on. It's got to be believable. A cat in a bag is believable, with physics and weight it is plausible. If you had a cat and you needed to carry it on a bus or something, it would be possible to stick it in a bag. But it would put up a hell of a fight. That's the point of the saying. But an elephant? A basket? Just doesn't work in the context as a metaphor. Even if you could build or weave a basket big enough to house an elephant, it would be game over in no time at all, wouldn't it? And in any case, we already have a perfectly good metaphor for a secret being let out.

Do we?

Yes. Letting the cat out of the bag.

Ah......

So is there any other possible explanation linguistically?

I like to think you could create a metaphor, or explain it away as an old Indian saying, translated, that 'the elephant is out of its basket'.

Well that is a bit of a stretch? What would that mean? We have already established a basket is not a feasible container for an elephant. So why are you harping on about it again?

Well what about that other saying, 'the woman is a basket case'. Could we not borrow that sense and make it work?

What is a basket case?

Someone who has lost their mind, is psychiatrically ill, it is slang for such unfortunate circumstances. 'Street lingo' if you will in reference to mental illness.

But where is the origin? Why must these damn baskets keep appearing. I feel I am losing my mind over this.......

Well traditionally when someone was institutionalised due to a breakdown, or needed to go to day therapy, basket weaving was a soothing activity of choice. Thus the combination of the person being 'a case' as in a medical issue, and basket, meaning they had lost their marbles and were now basket weaving.

Lost their marbles?

Oh this is taking too long.

Lost their marbles?

Lost their mind. It means lost their mind. So if you cannot keep hold of a load of marbles, they are scattering all over the floor, it describes how someone feels when they are in the grip of mental illnesss.

But I thought you said they were a basket case?

No, no, it is more complicated than that. The marbles metaphor is from the view of the subject, how they experience their mind. The basket case is from an observer's point of view, looking at someone who has lost their marbles, seeing them engage in basket weaving.

Oh I see, so it is a matter of perspective too. A subject and an object.

Indeed. So the elephant is being viewed as an object. And it is out of its basket. Meaning it has lost its mind. But again this doesn't work because an elephant would not be basket weaving. It would be impossible with its great big leathery legs. No, with the best will in the world this metaphor would not work.

So how could we change a word to make it work then? What about putting jungle instead of basket. So 'the elephant is out of the jungle'. That could be a metaphor for lots of things, couldn't it. I mean jungle works with elephant immediately. We have the right schema for the animal. The right associations. But it could be a metaphor for someone feeling at home in a place. It could imply that someone feels out of sorts.

Yes I like this. I remember a Texan guy saying to me, that living in Luxembourg, he felt so out of place, that he felt like he was dying on the vine. Said with a very Texan accent. I always remembered him saying this. Dying on the vine, he drawled.

New definition:

The elephant is out of the jungle means someone feels out of place.

Dylan Harris

Untitled

                                ok
let's be serious
that's not how i learn

asking me to repeat
until i know it solid
        a phrase

it's like
asking a dog
                to sing

i need to use the words
    in reality
a genuine act

ho ho ho
all the world's a stage
          but
              here
                  yes

i want to learn your language
    your headspace homeland
                         you

           if we're going to stick
which feels now
like throwing a five & a six
               with die loaded
                  for twos

i have to know why
you put up with
my stupidity
my horrible habits
the kind of thing
    that'd make
        the average rat
            dive into
                the snake's
                    jaw

open
                            jaw

        wide
                        wide
                        open
        jaw

isn't
the letter j
beautiful

the curve
        the curve
the letter j

beautiful   j

                beautiful

jump

Pierre Joris

A Glottal Choice

Why, how, to write in a language that is not the one called the mother tongue? I was born between languages, speaking Lëtzebuergesch, a dialect of the western Rhineland and the Moselle river valley, from MHG with Frankish roots. Not a dialect, a language, a langue, a tongue, a mother tongue I was never taught how to write – and whose passage from spoken dialect into codified, standard written form happened, unknown to me, during my passage through the scholastic institutions, to burst into an irredentist yet useful tool for a local literature when I had already turned my back & gone West to write in my fourth – but I am getting ahead of myself.

I learned how to read and write in German and French, in that order.

At fifteen I met English – no, wrong: I met V, the first woman with whom I was madly in love, and as chance had it, she was English. A summer and then that from which writing has its origin: separation, dispersal, distance. Distance through which to reach with writing. For her I wrote letters & poems in her language. For why should language be nailed to the old familial cross, cathexed to the mummy-daddy knot, the mother-tongue and father-land, nineteenth century nation-state-ism and "depth"-psychology, that control-Janus trying to turn what Ed Dorn called "the outside real and the insidereal" into stuffy claustro phobic Victorian spaces? Why should the great language moment not rather be the moment of the discovery of the other, the moment when our own sex speaks out, reaches out, rather than that of our progenitors?

At any rate, one always writes in a foreign language. Be it mother tongue or foreign language, language is always foreign, other, second — & only therefore can one find a home therein. All writing, all poetry is a trek towards language, our other, the station, the staying on the passage through time, I am a space traveler trying to write myself into an oasis corner, an amen corner as I circum-ambulate the polis of my life span, stopping here and there. Yet even that station, that *mawqif* is never a given, but always a wrestling so as to expulse the slag, to burn the dead wood and rearrange the stones in the ruins of the old camp. For all poetry rewrites language against itself.

So I was in love with her who was the way she spoke, and I thus was in love with English. A glottal choice imposed itself. It happened slowly: after those first letters & poems in English, the youth turned back for heat to what was at hand, leading to a return to writing in German and French for 2 or 3 years. But in the heart of Europe, a Europe that since '45 had become a "Quasi-Protektorat" (to use a German word from the hotter, later moments of that decade) of the US, American was fast becoming the culturally hip space for a teenager: rock 'n roll on Radio Luxembourg, Playboy magazine from the Bitburg PX, jazz over AFN radio stations, blue-jeans or "Texas-boxen" as our parents called them. And, of course there was the cinema, in the original language with French and Flemish subtitles: Yankee movies in my grand-mother's now full pre-war theater where once grand-father Joseph had shown Abel Gance's films to himself alone, we all now ate Hollywood from Audie Murphy oaters to James Dean's *Rebel Without a Cause,* and read Mickey Spillane novels, experienced ritual WWII Remembrance days with US army participation (my home town, Ettelbruck, was also known as "Patton town" for the hero of the Rundstedt whose troops had freed this area from the Germans, shelling the town for days on end and in the process burning my grand-father's large library and correspondence to the ground). Fifteen years later, on a beach in Spain, a young English honeymooning couple forgot a paperback in the sand, which I picked up: *On the Road* by Jack Kerouac. In the short-lived gay bookshop in the capital, Luxembourg, looking for erotica in Maurice Girodias' green "Traveler's Companion" series, I bought by mistake Allen Ginsberg's *Howl* and William Burroughs' *Naked Lunch.* I would take two or three years to be able to read that one.

(But to say that my writing moved between German, French and English is already somehow mistaken: years earlier my very first writings happened in totally different languages or in a language still more radically other: I spent my time scouring Karl May's travel and adventure novels, copying out the Mescalero Apache, Sioux, Comanche, Arab, Persian, Russian, Spanish, American language microliths embedded in the 72 volumes. From this perfectly hetero-geneous language matter I shaped my first writings which were hero-lists, kinship-lines, tribal schemata, ready-made sentences for explorers and nomadic wanderers, expletives, etcetera. I had name Nikunta, Hadji Halef Omar, Tatanka Yotanka, Winnetou, Gall…)

All of which stood me in good stead when, at nineteen, in Paris, I discovered Eliot and through him most quickly came to Ezra Pound's Cantos in George Whitman's Shakespeare & Company bookshop, where I sat nightly reading and wondering if I should quit medical school where I spent my days dissecting corpses, staining microtomed slices of animal tissue, reading in Rouvière's 3-volume *Anatomie* (which even now lies open downstairs on Nicole's desk, yielding bone drawings for her *Cantata* series). Reading Langston Hughes, Bob Kaufman, Allen Ginsberg, confirmed my sense of the intensity of the present, of a wild liveliness in the world my European upbringing had tried to hide. Reading Pound made me understand that poetry was a full-time, life-long occupation, not a genteel activity for rainy weekends. I had known what poetry was since that day in high school when a teacher had brought in someone who read contemporary German poems to us, and among them Paul Celan's "Death Fugue." My reaction had been instant, epidermic, total: the hairs on my arms literally stood up, an electric shock never before experienced coursed through my body, my breath stopped and when it started again it came from and into someone radically different. From that moment on I knew that there was a use of language different from and more powerful than all others, and it was sometimes called poetry. Now, in Paris I knew that that was what I wanted to do and that the only language in which I could do it was English. And thus I moved to New York, upstate, to learn and write, in the fall of 1967.

[An earlier version of this essay was published in Pierre Joris' collection of essays, *A Nomad Poetics*, Wesleyan UP, 2003]

Biographical Notices

Terry Adams was born in Tullamore, County Offaly, Ireland on the 15th March 1957. He is married with three daughters. Terry has lived in Luxembourg since 1990. He began writing after the death of his father in 1976 and has penned novels, collections of short stories and books of poetry. His true passion is poetry, a passion passed on to him by his father. His latest book *From Verdun to the Somme,* his eleventh, is another collection of poetry. Even after so many years living abroad, Tullamore and its people still feature in many of the pieces.

Susan Alexander is a native New Yorker and that remains a core part of her identity. She came to Luxembourg from Wall Street in 1989 to work in a bank. Hated the bank job. Loved Luxembourg. She is still here.

She has had a non-linear career path. She is a graduate of Wellesley College (Hillary Clinton is a classmate) and Princeton Theological Seminary (She is an ordained Presbyterian minister). She recently (2018) completed a PhD in Social Sciences. Her thesis topic: Intellectual Capital and the Future of Luxembourg. In between her B.A. and PhD, she spent three years as a psychotherapeutic resident at a New York City psychiatric clinic, headed Derivative, Fixed Income and International Securities Research at a Wall Street investment bank, co-founded a web site and web application development company and launched her own independent research firm. She is currently working as an expert for the European Commission, assessing public policy and funding proposals. She has authored thirteen books and is working on a trilogy set in Luxembourg. Her writing tends to focus on women who have led complex and interesting lives, their relationships and the choices they have made.

Jess Bauldry was born in 1980. She is British (and soon Luxembourgish). She has worked as a journalist since 2005 but her love of creative writing dates back to childhood. She has had short stories published in a UK anthology and two UK literary publications. She writes firstly for herself because she loves exploring how things could have turned out if this or that had happened – a sort of escape.

Jessica Becker was born in Luxembourg on July 2, 1982, and has dual citizenship in Luxembourg and the United States. After finishing high school in Luxembourg, she went on to study literature in Washington, DC, and complete a PhD in Hispanic Languages and Literatures at the University of California, Berkeley. Her poetry has been published in the United States and in Brazil. She currently resides in Alameda, California.

Catherine Bennett has recently retired from her work as a psychotherapist with her own cabinet here in Luxembourg. She has worked for years within the mental health sphere, having started with the NSPCC and the National Childbirth Trust as fundraiser and counsellor.

Her first published work was when she was 8 years old in The Puffin Club magazine with her poem 'Sizzling Snakes'. Since that time she has written stories, diaries, novellas and novels. She has yet to break out into the publishing world, but her retirement gives her the time to realise this ambition.

She is currently working on a book about cultural and historical responses to death. This intrigues her from a psychological and sociological perspective.

Her other work, more or less complete, is an autobiographical work, entitled *Desperate Housewives of Luxembourg*. It is intended to be funny, not just for those who star in it, but to others as well!

Jodie Dalgleish Born on 11 July 1968, Jodie holds dual citizenship in New Zealand and Ireland. She has been widely published in the South Pacific as a curator and critic of contemporary art and literature. There, she was also a finalist, and winner, of local short story contests, while also the author of a periodic arts column in a local newspaper. Before leaving New Zealand in 2015, she completed a Master of Creative Writing and held a six-month writer's residency at NZ Pacific Studio. In Europe – where she has dedicated herself to writing full-time – Jodie has continued to be published as an essayist, specifically for *Contemporary Hum,* a Paris-based online platform dedicated to NZ arts in a global context, and *Landfall,* the South Pacific's leading literary journal. She is also writing in response to her new home of Luxembourg and exploring European modes of storytelling more generally. In addition to creating collections of poetry and stories, she is also currently writing a novella and novel set in Luxembourg.

Shehzar Doja Syed Shehzar M. Doja was born in Dhaka, Bangladesh, and currently resides in Luxembourg as a poet and founder/editor-in-chief of the literary journal *The Luxembourg Review.* As a resident of Luxembourg, he was selected to represent the country (with Jean Portante) on a pan-European platform for a festival project commissioned for the city of Amsterdam. His work has appeared in numerous publications worldwide (*New Welsh Review, The San Antonio Review, Dhaka Tribune: Arts&Letters, Delano, Monsoon Letters, Sticks and Stones* etc) and has won places in several literary and a theatrical competition (1st prize for *The Madman's Lament* – which he wrote, acted in, & directed – in the Symbiosis Festival, Pune, India). He was a featured poet in 'SpokenWord Paris' in 2016 & a *NewAge* (newspaper) 'Youth Icon' in 2017. He was on the Jury Panel for the Literary Prize at the *Printemps des Poètes* festival in Luxembourg, 2018 and is currently working on an upcoming book project on the Rohingya community. His first book *Drift* (edited by Sudeep Sen) was published by UPL/Monsoon Letters in 2016.

Ruth Dugdall Born on 16 June 1971, of British nationality, Ruth studied English Literature at Warwick University (UK) before training as a probation officer. She decided to concentrate on her writing career when her novel *The Woman Before Me* won the 2005 Crime Writers' Association Debut Dagger. Her novels are informed by her direct experiences working within the Criminal Justice System and are published internationally. She lived in Luxembourg between 2014 and 2016, during which time she wrote and published *Nowhere Girl,* a crime thriller about human trafficking, set in the city. She currently lives in California, and is working on her eight novel.

Joanna Easter was born in Wales in 1996 to a Luxembourgish mother and a British father. She has been writing stories for as long as she can remember writing anything at all, her literary career starting out with her illustrious work *The Pumpkin Who Ran Away,* an unsurprisingly titled story about a pumpkin who ran away, written by the author when she was seven years old and hand-stapled together into a small volume with orange cardboard covers. Since then she has been a bookish child, a pedantic teenager, a depressed chemistry student, a slightly less depressed bookseller, a freelance gardener and a general layabout. She currently lives in a tent in the forest and is still writing stories, albeit generally ones of slightly more challenging subject matter.

Tullio Forgiarini was born in Luxembourg in 1966. His father is Italian, his mother Luxembourgish. He studied history in Luxembourg and Strasbourg (specialisation: Ancient History), and has been working as a teacher at Lycée du Nord in Wiltz since 1989. Forgiarini has written several novels, mostly dark, sarcastic, satirical, humorous 'neo-noir' crime fiction in French: *Miss Mona* (2000); *La Ballade de Lucienne Jourdain* (2001, 2016), *Carcasses* (2004), *Karnaval* (2005), *La deuxième mort de Ernesto Guevara de la Serna dit le Che* (2007). *Amok* (2011), a trashy, tragic road movie, is his first novel in Luxembourgish. It is based on his work with school drop-outs or traumatised adolescents. *Amok* was awarded the European Union Prize for Literature in 2013 and adapted to the screen as *Baby(a)lone* by Donato Rotunno in 2015. In 2016, Forgiarini published *De Ritter an der Kartonsrüstung,* a philosophical tale for children. His play *Du ciel,* a fierce and hilarious look at our attitude towards refugees, opened the season of Théâtre Ouvert de Luxembourg in October/November 2016. *Lizardqueen,* his first novel in German, was published at the same time. Forgiarini writes reviews and columns for different papers; he is a regular contributor to the satirical weekly *Feierkrop.*

Françoise Glod was born in Luxembourg in 1980. She studied English and American literature and theory in the UK. During this time, she also did a course in creative writing. She now works as an English teacher in Luxembourg City.

Dylan Harris (dylanharris.org) was born in Burton-in-Trent, UK, just before Sputnik flew. His poetry collections include *Big Town Blues, Anticipating the Metaverse, the Liberation of [Placeholder]* (all published by The Knives, Forks and Spoons Press, Newton-le-Willows, UK), and *Antwerp* (published by wurm press, Dublin, Ireland). He operates corrupt press (corruptpress.com), and likes beer.

Tom Hengen was born 15 December 1973 in Luxembourg, and grew up in Dudelange. He studied English and American literature at the University of Wales in Aberystwyth, where he came into contact with a vibrant and and eclectic literary scene. Apart from attending a creative writing course at uni, he took part in organising and reading at a number of events in Aberystwyth and in Wales. He also co-founded and co-edited the university's *Interchange Poetry* magazine, and had a few of his poems published in various magazines.

After returning from the UK, he was awarded the Luxembourg National Literature Prize for his collection *Explorations in C* in 2011, which was published by Éditions Phi, and he has had other poems in print in a few national newspapers.

Pierre Joris Born 1946. While raised in Luxembourg, he has moved between Europe, the US & North Africa for over half a century now, publishing more than 50 books of poetry, essays, translations & anthologies — most recently, *Stations d'al-Hallaj* (translated by Habib Tengour; Apic Editions, Algiers, 2018); a translation of Egyptian poet Safaa *Fathy's Revolution Goes Through Walls* (SplitLevel, 2018); *The Book of U /Le livre des cormorans* (with Nicole Peyrafitte, 2017); *The Agony of I.B.* (a play commissioned & produced by the Théatre National du Luxembourg; Editions PHI, 2016); *An American Suite* (early poems; inpatient press 2016); *Barzakh: Poems 2000-2012* (Black Widow Press 2014); *Breathturn into Timestead: The Collected Later Poetry of Paul Celan* (FSG 2014); *A Voice full of Cities: The Collected Essays of Robert Kelly* (co-edited with Peter Cockelbergh; 2014, Contra Mundum Press) & *The University of California Book of North African Literature* (volume 4 in the Poems for the Millennium series, coedited with Habib Tengour, 2012).

Forthcoming are *Adonis & Pierre Joris: Conversations in the Pyrenees* (Contra Mundum Press, 2018), the two final volumes of his Paul Celan translations, *Microliths* (Posthumous prose) from attem-verlag (2018) & *The Collected Earlier Poetry* (FSG 2020), as well as a volume of essays, *Against Tyranny* (Alabama University Press, 2019) & a *Pierre Joris Reader* (BWP, 2020). When not on the road, he lives in Bay Ridge, Brooklyn, with his wife, multimedia *praticienne* Nicole Peyrafitte.

Jos Kayser Born 1964. Luxembourger. Author of *Prinzessin Charlotte* (Editions Schortgen, 2017), *D'Bomi ass dout* and *De Mann deen ëmmer laacht* (Editions Schortgen, 2018). Kayser writes in Luxembourgish, French and English.

Georges Kieffer was born 1 January 1962 in Luxembourg, works as a teacher of English and lives with his wife, kids and cats in Mondorf-les-Bains. He studied English, Spanish and Fine Arts at Stirling University, Scotland (Mphil in 2011).

He has published *Schierbelen* (1998, PHI – joint winner with Georges Hausemer's *Iwwer Waasser* of the *Concours Littéraire National* in 1997); *Eidel Aerm, wann d'Liewe mam Doud ufänkt* (2001, PHI essais, kollektiv); *D'Kaya* (2003, PHI); *Biergop, biergof* (2007, op der lay); *D'Mëtt vum Land* (2016, SNE éditions).

Jean-Marc Lantz was born in Luxembourg City in 1964. A French citizen by birth, he became a Luxembourger at the age of 18. He studied Anglo-American Literature in Aberystwyth (Wales) and has been teaching English since the early nineties. After numerous exhibitions of his paintings both at home and abroad he is now trying his hand at writing in English and Luxembourgish. An inveterate Southerner, Jean-Marc currently works at the Lycée de Garçons in Esch/Alzette and resides in sunny Bettembourg.

James Leader was born in 1964 in England. He has lived and worked as a teacher of English and French in North America, Latin America, the Middle East and Europe.

His poem 'Fear' won the Newdigate Prize for Poetry at Oxford University in 1984, a prize previously won by Matthew Arnold and Oscar Wilde. He was runner-up in the Ballymaloe International Poetry Competition with his poem 'Phoebe and the Troopship' which was selected by Billy Collins out of 3,400 poems from around the world. In 2012 he came second in the Luxembourg National Literature Competition with his short story 'Rendition'. His young-adult novel *The Venus Zone* won the annual Luxembourg National Literature Competition in 2016. His novel *The Mysteries of Gogos* has been a set text in the Belgian Baccalaureate, and his novel

Chickendance has been taught in Luxembourg. He has done literary translations of prose and poetry from French, Spanish, German, Greek, Italian. In 2018 his poem 'Goethe in Rome' was selected from over five thousand poems as a runner-up in the Gregory O'Donoghue International Poetry Prize.

Noëlle Manoni A Luxembourger, Noëlle was born on 12 February 1999. She passed her *Examen de fin d'études secondaires* at Lycée Classique de Diekirch (section A) in summer 2018 and intends to pursue further education at the Royal Military Academy in Brussels. Her poem 'Farewell' won the first prize in the Black Fountain Writing Competition for young people, *Young Voices*. It was also short-listed for the *Prix Laurence* in Bettembourg. She wrote the poem in remembrance of a horse (called Amazonia), a former show-jumping mare which died because of her age (32 years), after Noëlle had hoped she would find strength again during the summer holidays.

Agnes Marton Born in 1965, Agnes is a Hungarian-born poet, writer, librettist, Reviews Editor of The Ofi Press (Mexico), founding member of Phoneme Media (USA), Fellow of the Royal Society of Arts (UK). Recent publications include her collection *Captain Fly's Bucket List* and four chapbooks with Moria Books (USA). Her work is widely anthologized, some examples being: 'Alice – Ekphrasis at the British Library', 'Anthem: A Tribute to Leonard Cohen', 'Poems for Pussy Riot'. She won the National Poetry Day Competition in the UK, and an anthology she edited *(Estuary: A Confluence of Art and Poetry)* won the Saboteur Award. Her short story 'Marina di San Cresci' was called exceptional in the Disquiet Literary Contest (USA). Her opera (composer: Vasiliki Legaki) premiered in London. In the award-winning poetry exhibition project 'Guardian of the Edge' 33 accomplished visual artists responded to her poetry (The Court of Justice of the European Union, Luxembourg).

She has been a resident poet on a research boat in the Arctic Circle, at the Scott Polar Research Institute (The University of Cambridge, UK), and also in Ireland (the Tyrone Guthrie Centre), Iceland (Gullkistan – Residency for Creative People), Italy (La Macina Di San Cresci), Spain (Arreciado – Wool Symposium), Portugal (First Impression) and Canada (Ou Gallery; Ayatana Artists' Research Program). Her poem *Fish Speech, Remember?* was performed by the BBC Singers (composer: Dan Chappell).

Robbie Martzen was born in Luxembourg in 1969. He is currently working as a teacher in his native country, but keeps wondering what he might be doing in a parallel universe. He likes nature, animals, and sometimes people. He also enjoys writing about all of the above.

He has published a small number of poems and texts in anthologies and journals and has been long- and shortlisted in various competitions, such as the *Blue Nose Poet-of-the-Year Competition* in London ('Highly Commended Poet' in 1999) and the *Concours Littéraire National* in Luxembourg (shortlisted in 1996).

Claudine Muno Born in 1979, Claudine holds the Luxembourgish nationality. Her first book, *The moon of the big winds,* was published in 1996. She continued to write in German, French and Luxembourgish. The novel *frigo* won the *Prix Servais* in 2004. Her last publication was *Komm net kräischen* (2016). She also writes song lyrics, mostly in English, and played/still plays in several bands (The Luna boots, Monophona).

Jeffrey Palms was born in 1986 in the suburbs of Detroit, Michigan. In his twenties he lived in Dublin, Lisbon, Washington, Edinburgh, and Maastricht before settling in Luxembourg in 2015. He writes for the d'Lëtzebuerger Land on culture and the expat experience, and has had reviews and creative pieces published in the Luxembourg Times, HeadStuff, and Vulture. He is currently working on a collection of short stories.

Jeff Schinker was born in 1985 in Luxembourg. So far, he has published a book, *Retrouvailles*, as well as several short stories in Luxembourgish and French anthologies and magazines. He has written a play, *Theseus,* organizes several cycles of readings and works for the daily newspaper Tageblatt, where he is responsible for the cultural pages. Later this year, he'll publish a short story collection, which will be in four languages. He doesn't believe in sleep.

Lambert Schlechter was born in Luxembourg in December 1941. He is a retired teacher and lives in Wellenstein near the Moselle River. He has published some 30 books of poetry, essays, chronicles, short stories in Luxembourg, Québec, Belgium and above all in France. His work has been translated into Armenian, Bulgarian, Italian, Bosnian, English, Spanish and Arabic.

Le murmure du monde *Le Murmure du monde,* Le Castor astral, 2006; *La Trame des jours,* Les Vanneaux, 2010; *Le Fracas des nuages,* Le Castor astral, 2013; *Inévitables Bifurcations,* Les Doigs dans la prose, 2016; *Le Ressac du temps,* Les Vanneaux, 2016; *Monsieur Pinget saisit le râteau et traverse le potager,* Phi, 2017; *Une mite sous la semelle du Titien,* Tinbad, 2018.

Pieds de mouche *Pieds de mouche,* petites proses, Phi, 1990; *Le Silence inutile,* petites proses, Phi, 1991 / La Table ronde, 1996; *Ruine de parole,* roman schématique et sentimental, Phi, 1993.

Prose *Angle mort,* récit, Phi, 1988 / L'Escampette, 2005; *Partances,* nouvelles, L'Escampette, 2003; *Smoky,* chroniques, Le Temps qu'il fait, 2003; *Petits travaux dans la maison,* Phi / Ecrits des Forges, 2008; *Pourquoi le merle de Breughel n'est peut-être qu'un corbeau,* Estuaires, 2008; *La Robe de nudité,* petites proses, Vanneaux, coll. Amorosa, 2008: *Lettres à Chen Fou,* et autres proseries, L'escampette, 2011; *La pivoine de Cervantès,* et autres proseries, La Part commune, 2011.

Poetry *Das grosse Rasenstück,* Lyrik, Guy Binsfeld, 1982; *La Muse démuselée,* Phi, 1982; *Honda rouge et cent pigeons,* Phi, coll. graphiti, 1994; *Le Papillon de Solutré,* quatrains, Phi, coll. graphiti, 2003; *L'Envers de tous les endroits,* Phi, coll. graphiti, 2010; *Les Repentirs de Froberger,* quatrains biographiques, La Part des anges, 2011; *Piéton sur la voie lactée,* 99 neuvains, Phi, coll. graphiti, 2012; *Enculer la camarde,* 99 neuvains, Phi, coll. graphiti, 2013; *Je est un pronom sans conséquence,* 99 neuvains, Phi, coll. graphiti, 2014; *La Théorie de l'univers, distiques décasyllabiques,* Phi, coll. graphiti, 2015; *Milliards de manières de mourir,* 99 neuvains, Phi, coll. graphiti, 2016; Anthologie personnelle *Nichts kapiert, doch alles notiert,* Lyrik & Prosa, 1968-2014, Binsfeld, 2014; *one day I will write a poem,* Black Fountain Press, 2018.

Sandra Schmit Born in 1972, Sandra is a literary researcher, translator and writer. She has an MA in Medieval English and French literature and works at the Luxembourg Literary Archives in Mersch, where she is part of the team responsible for the online dictionary of Luxembourg authors. She has co-curated exhibitions on Luxembourg literature and published two commented editions of literary classics as well as an English translation of 19th century Luxembourg-American poetry, *Prairie Flowers.* Her first novel, *A Winter Tale,* was published in 2005, followed by its sequel, *Rights of Spring,* in 2011. She has received great acclaim for her translation of Guy Rewening's *Your Heart of Ice is Hot as Vice* (Éditions Guy Binsfeld, 2017).

Robert Schofield Born in 1963, Robert grew up in Southampton, on the south coast of England, and then studied languages at Oxford, coupled with sporadic working in a German electronics factory, and milking sheep for Roquefort cheese.

He then started a long career in banking, first in the UK and in Africa, and now in Luxembourg. He has also been writing fiction for the best part of two decades.

His first novel, *The Fig Tree and the Mulberry,* was a prize-winner in Luxembourg's *Concours littéraire national,* and was published by Éditions Saint-Paul. It tells a story from a forgotten part of the second world war, when children from British cities were evacuated alone overseas, in this case to New Zealand, to escape the threat of invasion. His children's book *The Hoogen-Stoogen Tulip,* including satirical drawings from the Luxembourg illustrator Carlo Schmitz, was published by Editions Guy Binsfeld in 2013, both in English and in Luxembourgish, and was shortlisted for the annual children's book prize. It tells the story of the first supposedly black tulip, coveted and bought by Fattmann van Biggestbanken, the most powerful merchant in all Amsterdam. Chaos ensues when the tulip blooms and is revealed to be not quite what it seemed.

Cecile Somers is a copy writer and voice artist best known for telling people "The person you are trying to call, is not available right now".

Cecile Somers was born in the Netherlands in 1963, but grew up in Luxembourg where she attended the European School. She studied English Literature and Linguistics at Leiden University, and followed several writing workshops, which led to the publication of her first children's book *Vijf citroenen en een varkentje* (De Bezige Bij, Amsterdam). She is an IMDB-listed scriptwriter, having written the scripts for animated films *The Golden Horse* and *Apple Pie, The King & I* (in production). A member of the Creative Writing

Group Luxembourg she is currently working on a screenplay starring cleaning ladies and librarians, and trying to finish her underground cult novel *Cornflakes For The Underworld* (formerly known as *The Cactus Chronicles),* about people living inside the Cactus supermarket at Belle Étoile. It's an underground cult novel because many people have heard about the book but very few have actually read it (the latter on account of it still being unfinished).

Wendy Winn is a writer, poet, journalist, artist, radio show presenter, yoga enthusiast who is naturally curious and appreciative of the world around her and tries to capture some of what she sees and feels in writing and in art. She has a bachelor's degree in English and a master's degree in creative writing. She was formerly the editor of Luxembourg's only English newspaper at the time. She is now the web editor of the European Commission's public health letter (which reaches over 23,000 readers), a freelance journalist and a radio presenter, but she's always written fiction and poetry too. She has had several short stories and poems published, some of which were awarded prizes, and she has had two short plays performed on stage. One day she may even get her novels out of the drawer and edit them, and she'll certainly write new ones.

Appendix

What does writing
in English mean to you?
Why do you write
in English?

Susan Alexander The obvious answer is, of course, because I am a native English speaker. However, being a native speaker is no guarantee that one writes well. I have worked quite hard at my writing and developing a style and give a lot of credit to Miss Jackson ("the Ax"), my high school English teacher.

Although in my adolescence I did write some poetry in French (I blame Baudelaire), most of my language studies have been in "dead" languages – Sanskrit, Hebrew, Greek, Latin. I could not read a newspaper in Athens or in Tel Aviv. I am proud that, for most of my adult life, I have been paid for my writing, whether it was for a sermon, web site content, a marketing brochure or a financial market research report.

I love English because it can be very concise. One can remove extraneous words the way a sculptor chips away at a block of marble to reveal the figure hidden within. English also has natural rhythms of which I am very conscious, and I speak my words to myself while I write.

While I embrace English as a living language (I am fine with "google" as a verb), I deplore the tyranny of political correctness that insists, for example, that actresses be called actors (in that case, why not call actors, actresses?). Rather than the inelegant "he or she" I prefer the inclusive "he." And will happily "man" the barricades for this cause.

Jess Bauldry I write in English because it's my native tongue. I grew up in a small village in the south east of England, which doesn't feel so far away as the people and countryside always find a way into my writing. I also think I have more interesting things to say when I use English than when I use French or Luxembourgish.

Jessica Becker I grew up in a bilingual home speaking English and Luxembourgish as my first languages. For me, reading literature in English felt like a magical escape from what I had to read for school, and when I discovered and fell in love with novelists like Vladimir Nabokov and Salman Rushdie as a teenager, I was inspired to explore the language as a writer.

Catherine Bennett I write in English because I am English. I was raised in London and as an adult have lived in London, Cambridge and for the last 14 years in Luxembourg. My husband is London Jamaican and we have two adult children, our son living near us in Luxembourg and our daughter in central London.

Jodie Dalgleish I feel very privileged to have grown up with English as my mother tongue and to now have the opportunity to live in another part of the world where I can hear, read and speak other languages. Writing in English – which evolved in a rich European context – brings my current world of experience together and allows me to connect across multiple locations and modes of life.

Why I write in English?

English is my mother tongue and provides me with the most intimate way of exploring the phenomenon of language. I find English to be a specific yet nuanced language (within the genre of poetry, in particular) while it is highly inflected by other European languages and enriched by a European philosophical and literary tradition. It gives me the opportunity to draw on a wide scope of linguistic experience and literature, while it allows me to experiment more freely.

Shehzar Doja I consider English to be my primary language as my entire educational process and upbringing was centered around it. However, what drove me to write in English from a very young age is my love for the English and Irish poets. A poem like 'Sea-Fever' by John Masefield from a very young age imbued a sense of wanderlust in me and as such, I continued to traverse the unexplored corners of my imagination with the same language.

Françoise Glod I write in English because in other languages I often feel at a loss for words whereas in English I can lose myself in the words.

Tom Hengen I suppose, at the start, writing in English was a kind of opening up to a world other than what I was familiar with, in order to escape a culture that I had difficulties finding a place in. Now it has become a quest for exploring the world and my own mind within it.

English is the colour I have chosen to paint my pictures with, I suppose. Or possibly, it's the language that has chosen me, as it seems to come more naturally to me than any other language. English is such a rich language and begs for the writer to delve into it and use it creatively.

Jos Kayser English is for me the ideal language for short stories. I also feel that ambiguity and dark humour work best in English.

Georges Kieffer At school my first mark in English was a lousy 7 out of 60 marks. Ever since then, I have tried to improve. "A Bigger Splash" is my first effort in the Bard's language! So writing in English could mean overcoming some sense of inferiority complex, plus it's simply a beautiful language! I normally write in Luxembourgish. One idea is to translate my four novels from Luxembourgish into English...

Jean-Marc Lantz I love writing in English because some things simply cannot be said in another language. For those of us who have spent a considerable time away from the gilded cage and may even have found a second home abroad, writing in English keeps the flame of adventure alight, opens the doors of perception and widens the horizon. Writing is about sharing experiences and connecting the past with the present to hopefully summon a viable future. Being creative in as many languages as possible keeps us on our toes and the spectres of death and oblivion at bay. It is life.

Agnes Marton I switched into writing in English while I studied at the University of Denver Publishing Institute. I enjoy recreating the language playfully (using non-existent words, distortions, unusual punctuation and layout, multilingual bits, juxtaposition).

Robbie Martzen I write in English because the words usually know what I want to say long before I do.

Claudine Muno I became interested in the English language through songs and films because I was eager to understand what was being sung/said. In 1993 I saw *The Remains of the Day,* which I loved and I began to watch all the Merchant-Ivorys and tried to read E.M. Forster's novels. I took a year of English at the Centre universitaire de Luxembourg and still mainly read English literature.

Jeff Schinker Writing in English means exploring new linguistic horizons. It's a challenge, for I'm rather used to writing in French. It implies taking advantage of the multicultural landscapes in Luxembourg as well as delving into yet another syntax and exploring different stylistic ways and possibilities of telling a story. It's also an opportunity not to get stuck inside one single (linguistic) habitus, but to see how style evolves when we change the language we write in.

Sandra Schmit Luxembourgish is certainly my mother tongue, but some time in secondary school, I adopted English as my "literary mother tongue", as I much prefer to read literature, news, science mags or anything else really in English. And what you read unerringly shapes your mind. I speak German and French well, as many Luxembourgers do, but I feel more at home with English. When I look for the perfect, poignant expression, which conveys just what I want to say, I turn to the language of Wordsworth and Wilde. Yes, I can walk in many shoes, but when I dance, I dance in English.